The Three Deaths of Giovanni Fumiani

6/9/23

For Leslie
The best Reader & sister
a brother could have.

Love,

The Three Deaths
of Giovanni Fumiani

Jeffrey Hantover

Cuidono • Brooklyn

The Three Deaths of Giovanni Fumiani
© 2023 Jeffrey Hantover

This is an advance reader's edition set from uncorrected proofs.
Type, design, and layout are not final.
Dates and prices are subject to change without notice.

Fiction • May 2023 • 978-1-944453-22-0 • $17.00 • 210 pages
ebook 978-1-944453-23-7 • $8.99
Publicity: publicity@cuidono.com
Sales: sales@cuidono.com

Cover image: Sara Nalle

Cuidono Press
Brooklyn NY
www.cuidono.com

For Mee-Seen

I

The First Death of Giovanni Fumiani

Venice, 1706

Angels swirled in heavenly ecstasy above the cold, hard marble floor of the church of San Pantalon. Candles flickered and wisped in the side chapels. Father Zampelli stood in front of the church and looked up. He smiled at the glorious vision he had promised God. Come down, he wanted to say, it's perfect. The man high above him on the scaffold had his back turned and did not see the priest wave goodnight.

Clutching a brush in his hand, he took a step back to better see if anything more needed to be done. The wooden planks of the scaffold creaked and shifted under his boots. He felt the cool air of fluttering angel wings against his checks. His paint splattered smock billowed in the air. Neither the martyred saint nor God's angels could save him.

Blood edged the fallen man's head, trickling around his shoulders like the feathery tips of an angel's wings. Giovanni Fumiani crouched over the fallen man. He knew without touching the man's cheek or the veins of his neck. He looked up at the ceiling. Saint Pantalon, the Holy Helper, healer of body and soul, the all compassionate, looked down in silence. It was too late. Nothing more could be done. He rose a ghost and disappeared into the night.

II

The Second Death of Giovanni Fumiani

1

He lay face up on the floor, hands at his sides. A stench stronger than the Giudecca Canal on a humid August afternoon filled the small room. The butcher who lived on the floor below and the priest from San Eufemia pressed scented handkerchiefs against their noses and mouths. They guessed he had been dead two days or more. The butcher's young son threw open the latched shutters. There was no sign of foul play, just an old man dead from a bad heart or the toll of age. The butcher pulled the gray blanket from the bed to cover the body. The dead man had a thick white beard and long hair almost touching his shoulders. He looked at the ceiling with the sweet smile of a saint who had lain down in a field to admire the stars. The priest followed the dead man's eyes to a solitary angel outlined in ochre chalk floating on the white plaster between the beams. A few simple lines and an angel so real the priest wanted to reach out and touch the soft soles of his feet. The priest swore the dead man was smiling at the angel, willing him upward. The butcher pulled the blanket up to the dead man's chin. The priest stared at the dead man's face. There was something about his eyes that seemed familiar. He mumbled a prayer through his handkerchief and made the sign of the cross over the dead man's pallid face. Before covering the body the priest looked up again at the ceiling. He was certain the angel was ascending, waiting for the ceiling to part, waiting to disappear into the golden light of heaven.

2

Stefano Bigio wiped bits of polenta from his chin with a frayed cotton napkin, careful to catch any drops before they stained his shirt. He didn't have enough shirts to be careless. When he went out, he could pull his patrician's robe tight across his chest to cover any spots, but knowing they were there, he would feel soiled. Father Zampelli's note lay on the table next to one of his three pewter plates. The priest's handwriting seemed hurried, unlike his usual fine hand. Whatever his reason for asking him to come to San Pantalon, the priest could wait. Bigio never rushed a good dish of warm polenta or gulped a cup of coffee.

"Patience, Saint Jude. You know I will save you some." The dusky sparrow, Bigio's constant companion, sat unmoving in his cage by the window, too tired of his life's unchanging view to sing or even bother to fluff and flutter his wings. Bigio ate slowly, savoring each spoonful between his tongue and the roof of his mouth. He pushed Pliny's *Natural History* aside to concentrate all his senses on his one true meal of the day.

Born with a deformed hip and right leg two inches shorter than the left, he always moved slowly, even with the special heels cobblers fixed to his shoes. He was a man of sixty-nine, still with a full head of gray hair – he thought a periwig an effeminate French fashion. He had an aquiline nose and the angular features of his patrician line made more pronounced by his meager living. Almost six feet when he stood straight, Bigio walked more slowly than patricians with strong, well-formed legs who strode deliberately in long black robes through the narrow streets of the city. Bigio never scurried to keep up. That would have been unmanly and only drawn attention to his deformity. He thought it unseemly for a patrician, whatever his straitened circumstances, to call attention to himself. If anything, he walked slower than he could – a lame man's stratagem to silently command. Others were forced to slow down to keep at his side. He couldn't study someone's face or measure their words looking at their back. The slower they walked, the easier it was to observe them. Bigio was good at observing. To make his way in a city of masks, a cripple had to learn to read the eyes and soul behind the mask of politeness that pretended compassion but was only relief at being born full-fingered and firm limbed.

His destiny was set once the old midwife who brought his father into the world ran her hand along his malformed hip and leg. He would be the son who wouldn't marry. Whatever patrimony his father didn't gamble away or spend on lavish banquets, hunting parties at summer estates along the Brenta, and the daily extravagances of maintaining a noble appearance would go to the second son that his father prayed would be born with well-shaped limbs and a hardy constitution. Gregorio, born two years later, was the normal son chosen to marry and preserve the family line. Gregorio lived with his wife and two young daughters in the high-ceilinged rooms on the first and second floors of the family palazzo, while Bigio clomped to his room on the top floor.

Bigio once ate off enameled plates and drank from goblets studded with gems, while canaries, turtledoves, and rainbow colored birds twitted and trilled in cages next to hanging baskets of fresh flowers and fragrant herbs. One Christmas feast liveried servants brought salvers of pasties to the table and cut them open with solemn flourish. Birds burst from the warm crust and flew up into the beamed ceiling and out the open windows into the cold night air. His clothes, scented and folded, once lay in gilded chests. He never wore the same shirt and stockings twice in a week. Now he lived in San Barnaba with other impoverished patricians on the charity of the Republic, his home two sparse rooms in a damp and decaying palazzo. His small inheritance had disappeared into his courtesan's purse and the café coffers of San Marco. All that he had left was the family name, an old man's toenails like his father's, yellow and hard as a tortoise's shell, and a small treasure of books he never remembered his father reading. Their leather bindings and covers were cracked and warped, and their pages foxed from the moist Venetian air. He sat at his table in the dim light of day and in flickering candlelight, reading and rereading the histories of Pliny, Suetonius, Polybius, and Plutarch. He slept on a narrow bed, ate boiled greens and street mongers' watery mussel soup from a pewter plate and bowl bent and scratched, and kept stockings in need of darning in a painted chest faded and chipped. Poorly tended, the vineyard had gone fallow, and Bigio was the last drop of a good vintage.

When he was a young boy, his father dressed when the rest of world went to sleep. He leaned over his son's bed, tousled his hair, patted his check with soft hands, and kissed him on the forehead "for good luck" before striding off to the Ridotto at San Moisè with a gambler's blind confidence that this night the odds would be in his favor. His father left the casino most nights with his purse empty but his good name unsullied. Bigio's father always paid his gambling debts promptly and was generous with those who on occasion owed him money. On the rare mornings after the dice had tumbled his father's way, Bigio found a silver ducat resting beneath his silk pillow. Now he never slept through the night – getting up only twice to piss in the chamber pot was a victory – and awoke to find another few gray hairs on his rough cotton pillow.

Bigio's father was an honest man who, for all his intemperance and folly, was a bitter enemy of falsehood and an expert in the detection of lies. His father wanted to toughen up his lame son for the life that lay ahead. If he caught him in a lie, whether from a false tone of voice, a stutter, or guilty glance, Stefano got his ears boxed, no matter his youth or lameness, more often and more severely than his brother. When he was ten, he couldn't wait to see the Carnival jugglers and puppeteers in San Marco. He sprinkled water on his forehead and reddened his cheeks with a cloth warmed on the fireplace andirons. His tutor, a gullible young man from Paris, was deceived by his feigned fever and told him to say his prayers and rest quietly in bed for the day. When the tutor closed the door, young Stefano stuffed pillows under the blanket and made a wall of pillows to hide where his head should have rested. His father caught him sneaking back at dusk. He took a belt to his son's bare buttocks. "If you had been honest and asked, I would have let you go," his father said.

Rough winds and foul weather made no allowances for well-formed patricians. His brother was lost off the coast of Crete on a diplomatic mission for the Republic. While he was alive, his wife carped that the paltry inheritance her father-in-law had bequeathed Bigio was much too generous, and the meager allowance her husband gave his brother was a burdensome extravagance that robbed their daughters' dowries and threatened their future matches with other noble families. In widow's weeds she barely tolerated his presence. She drew the purse strings tighter and tighter and made him feel like an interloper in the family palazzo. Her constant glower and vinegary tongue drove him out to live alone in San Barnaba among other poor patricians.

Bigio took another spoonful of polenta. On chilly winter mornings when he was a boy, he snuck into the kitchen to watch the ancient family cook make polenta. A bug-eyed woman, who looked as if she were in a state of constant surprise, she was a gentle soul kind to a lame boy. She stirred the thickening polenta from bottom to top with a long handled wooden spoon for what seemed like hours to his empty stomach. Scraping the cornmeal from the sides of a copper kettle so it would not burn, she told him to watch out for clumps, as if a patrician's son would ever make his own polenta. Finally, she swirled a thick slice of butter into the middle of his bowl and sprinkled bits of Parmesan over the polenta. He still remembered the feel of the warm bowl between his hands.

Every few days the cook's niece, now herself an old woman, secretly spooned a dish of polenta in the kitchen of his youth and sent the kitchen boy scurrying across the Rialto Bridge to deliver the polenta, still warm, to Bigio. He scraped the bowl with a piece of brown bread. He barely remembered the taste of white bread. Bigio tore off a morsel of the bread. He held it between his fingers and opened the cage to feed the sparrow. "Your patience has paid off my dear friend. Patience is a virtue. You and I bear this world with great and endless patience, don't we Jude?"

When the old patrician across the hall died four years before, none of the neighbors wanted to care for the drab bird that sang infrequently and dully. Bigio knew what it was like to be unwanted and took the bird in. Bigio named him Saint Jude. A lost cause, Bigio needed a feathered saint to look after him. He fed him scraps of stale bread and an occasional dead fly or water bug. The bird was a patient listener to Bigio's complaints about his aches and pains and the spiraling decline of the Serene Republic.

3

The bloated body floated under the short bridge leading to Campo Santa Margherita. A cluster of ragged boys, apprentices on their errands in patched pantaloons and worn tunics, and a few old women stood at the canal's edge peering into the dark water. Two of the boys threw rotten apples at the body as the current carried it by. Bigio glanced at the young man, his long hair fanning out beside his bruised face, and kept walking. This far from the Ducal Palace, he was probably the victim of some drunken argument or family vendetta, but it was wise not to show too much interest if spies from the Council of Ten were lurking nearby. The Council was the true ruler of the Republic, its secret tentacles extending throughout Venice. But the Council was usually more discrete – a weighted sack tossed into the lagoon on a cloudy night.

Bigio made his way past the fruit and vegetable stalls that filled the center of the wide campo, wagging his walking stick in front of him. He waved to the young daughter of his favorite fruit seller as he passed the stall. She smiled as she always did and waved back. He could get along without a walking stick but carried it as an instrument of intimidation. Most times all he had to do was call out, "Make way," put on a theatrical limp, and swing his foot in a shallow arc, and strangers gave the evil-omened cripple wide berth. The carved ivory handle, a Venetian lion once a vibrant white, was now yellowed with a visible crack running along its leonine snout. The cracked lion of Venice, how appropriate, he thought. The proud descendants of Troy, how far we have fallen.

13

The last time he remembered using his walking stick as a weapon was at last year's Festa della Sensa in the Piazza San Marco. He came to San Marco to listen to the café gossip of the fallen world and observe the citizens of the dying Republic. He had little patience for the forced jollity of the season, the drunken revelers, rowdy apprentices, the shoppers, and foreign gawkers crowding the temporary stalls and booths. The tradesmen and artisans of the Republic were all there: the goldsmiths, the mercers, the cobblers, the coppersmiths, tinsmiths, carpenters, glassmakers, mirror makers, and the sellers of alabaster, perfume, combs, paternoster beads, needles, swords, knives, second hand clothing, and images of the Holy Virgin. The young and curious circled buskers, jugglers, acrobats, snake charmers, mountebanks hawking elixirs and healing waters, and magicians in motley whose cut arms spouted blood one moment and the next were miraculously healed to the gasps of the gullible. Betrothed young women walked up and down the line of stalls with their mothers shopping for their trousseaus, while common folk scoured for their one cheap dress of the year. The piazza was full of foreigners who flocked to the city for the fair and the indulgences dispensed to anyone who visited the church of San Marco during the festivities. Out of the corner of his eye Bigio saw a young pickpocket lift a silk purse from a well-dressed citizen. He brought his walking stick down violently on the thief's wrist, and the purse fell to the ground. The pickpocket took the Savior's name in vain with a loud curse and darted into the dense crowd. Bigio knew firsthand that life was hard, and everyone had to live, but not at the expense of another, no matter his empty belly. A man had principles, otherwise he was no better than the ravenous wolves that prowled the forests along the Brenta.

The campo sentinels, three crones made sisters by age's alchemy, huddled by the five-sided wellhead near the middle of the campo. Their heads were crooked in conspiratorial conversation. Their eyes roamed their domain for suspect intruders while Bigio passed by them unnoticed, like a servant at a banquet thought deaf and dumb to the world outside his duties or a mute eunuch in the Turk's seraglio whose absence of one sense was believed to deprive him of all others. He limped through the city invisible to the sharpest-eyed merchant or Republic's spy.

For the three campo crones, the parish was their world. Like many of their neighbors, they never ventured across the Grand Canal into San Marco. Born, blessed, and soon to be mourned among these stones, this was their Venice. Here within the rectangular boundaries of the campo they lived their lives. Here they bought fruit, vegetables, pasta, flour, and cheap wine. Here they prayed and gossiped. For Bigio, despite his mismatched legs, the entire city was his home before he moved across the Grand Canal to San Barnaba.

He went every Sunday afternoon to the meeting of the Great Council in the Ducal Palace and would go until his scarlet robe was too threadbare for the daylight. It was his patrician duty, and what else was there for him to do on Sunday? His brother's widow never invited him for dinner and had turned his nieces against him. He had no children who honored him, no grandchildren to spoil. Instead he mingled among fellow patricians in the palace courtyard and lingered in Piazza San Marco over coffee and pastry – if someone offered to pay. He listened to the murmurings of the Republic: who was buying whose vote, what patrician of professed faith and fidelity had been seen entering the secret canal entrance to the home of a woman of unblemished reputation, what merchant whose fortune wrecked on the shoals of some foreign coast left the world of the sane to join the madmen of San Servolo, and who was falling on their knees with panting passion before a certain young nun in the convent of San Luca. He was deaf to the candied fruit sellers hawking their sweets in the Piazza and scabby boys whining for a coin. He listened, undisturbed by the sharp-eyed fortune tellers who read the present well enough to know his purse held more lint than coin and his tomorrow would be as empty and repetitious as today.

A slice of watermelon, a cold plate of polenta, a piece of yesterday's bread, and the kindness of the Republic. He scraped by, savoring the indulgence of an evening cup of thick coffee in San Marco. The waiters spoke to him with respect and sat him in a back table where he could sip his coffee and read the *Gazzetta* away from the loud chatter of foreigners. This was the life he led. He was a man with no illusions. He had earned his dim vision of the future. Nothing would change – it was too late. He had his books and Saint Jude to keep him company. He would die alone in his room with his honor and a good cup of coffee. God might not have abandoned him, but He obviously had more important matters to attend to.

A heavy-set man with a scraggly beard, thick tufted eyebrows, and salt and pepper hair wild as wind-swept wheat sat cross-legged on a dirty square of rough burlap at the foot of the bridge that led to campo San Pantalon. He was here every day, a sad-eyed mongrel crouched at his side. People said he was touched in the head for what reason no one seemed to know. He lost his wife and child in a fire and was never the same some said, others thought he was a soldier scarred by the horrors of war, while a few believed he was simply born a lost soul. He came from another parish to beg here without shaming whatever family he might still have. He plucked a battered lute and talked to his dog that listened without interruption or ridicule. A few coins lay between the dog's paws. Several young fops slowed down pretending to search their purses for a spare coin, and laughing, kept on walking. Bigio fished out two lonely coins from the leather pouch tied to the belt beneath his cloak and dropped them on the burlap.

4

"Fumiani is dead…again." Father Zampelli tugged on the wattles of stubbled flesh beneath his chin.

Fumiani's death had been the subject of many homilies on the mysterious ways of God. Bigio thought it a cruel joke. Giovanni Fumiani went to Bologna at fifteen to learn from the masters of quadratura how to create the illusion of an infinite heaven. He worked twenty years on the painting that stretched across the width and length of the ceiling in San Pantalon. Four years ago, at sixty-one, just as he was finishing the painting, he fell to his death from the scaffolding onto the marble floor.

Some said the ceiling of San Pantalon was the largest painting on canvas in the world. Bigio wouldn't know – he hadn't traveled the world. The farthest he had ever gone were the summer villas along the Brenta, and that was years ago when his father and brother were still alive. If he traveled far from Venice, it would not be to stare at church ceilings.

Fumiani was buried in one of the side chapels, and now Zampelli sat beneath the painter's illusionist masterwork, telling Bigio with a trembling voice that he was found dead again two days before in a small room on the Giudecca.

"So who's buried here?" Bigio swung his cane in a wide arc across the marble floor.

Zampelli shook his head. "Stefano, I don't know." The priest's thick lips quivered, his cheeks reddened.

"You don't know, after all these years?" A man lay unnamed four years without prayers for his soul. Bigio didn't need to wear a priest's cassock to know that was an offense against God.

"I thought he was Fumiani."

"You knew him a long time."

The words caught in Zampelli's throat, "Over thirty years." The priest had been the chaplain at the Scuola San Rocco when Fumiani, then thirty, completed the large painting of Saint Roch distributing his riches to the poor for the nave ceiling in the church of San Rocco. "When I looked up at that painting, I was standing there on the steps among the poor with their outstretched arms, watching the dear saint give away his wealth for the glory of God. When I came to San Pantalon, I promised Fumiani he would paint the ceiling when the church was rebuilt."

Zampelli leaned back, staring at the ceiling. "Stefano, he couldn't paint on plaster, because the damp air would eat it away. Fumiani told me it would take half a hundred or more pieces of canvas – enough canvas to sail a fleet of ships to the New World. He wanted to start as soon as he saw Comino's plans for the church. It would be like painting heaven itself, he said."

Everyone in Venice knew the work of the Republic's old masters – Bellini, Veronese, Titian, Tintoretto. Bigio knew them more by name and reputation than sight and treasured memory. He knew next to nothing of painters working now. They didn't come to his bare room seeking commissions. But even with his unschooled eye, he could see there was no other painting like this in Venice. "Couldn't you have told him to paint something less grand? Something that wouldn't have cost so much and taken so long?"

Zampelli swept his hand toward the few old women praying before the altar and lighting candles in the side chapels. "They are unlettered souls. They walk into the church, light a candle, say a prayer, and leave to go about their daily lives. The heresy from the North confuses them, sows doubt in their hearts. I want their faith to be firm as Toledo steel. I want the faithful to stand in awe beneath the glory of heaven." His eyes gleaming, he pointed to the painted ledges and balustrades. "Fumiani confused their eyes to strengthen their faith. He made the faithful question what was real and what was illusion. They tap the hard marble columns with their fingers and think they knew the real from the false. Then they look up, not sure what's marble and what's paint. Maybe the world they thought so real and permanent is an illusion, and the heaven of paint and canvas glowing above them is the true eternal reality."

Words, just words, Bigio thought, but he kept silent.

"They think the pagans above them are standing on solid ground. Then they look again and see they're tottering on the edge of the abyss. Without the wings of true faith, they too will tumble to their destruction. I know it sounds strange, Stefano, but illusion can reveal the truth."

Twenty years and thousands and thousands of ducats for timber, canvas, paint, and the labor of dozens of workmen. Did God really demand such an ambitious undertaking in his name? Couldn't the lesson be taught more cheaply through a few sermons? Bigio thought to himself.

"Didn't you know it wasn't him?"

"I couldn't bear to see his face after he fell from such a height. I wanted to remember him as he had been. I recognized his smock. All its streaks and stains." Zampelli pressed his fist against his lips, looked down at his feet and then up toward the ceiling. In the chapel of Saint Ann near the church entrance, a pregnant woman lit a candle. A white snake hovered in the air and disappeared into the shadows. "The painting was perfect, why did he go up again? What more could he do?" Zampelli shook his head side to side. "It was an accident. Everyone knew it. He must have stumbled."

"But he didn't." Bigio saw the pain in Zampelli's face as the priest played out in his mind the possibilities he didn't want to accept or even voice, the uncertainty he couldn't live with.

Zampelli looked down at the floor. "Someone died here. God wants us to find out who. Prayers must be said for him, Stefano. You can find out things. You're good at it."

Venice was a city of secrets. Patrician fathers counseled their children in the serpentine ways of secrecy as if it were the eleventh commandment. Merchants hoarded knowledge of ships' cargo and arrivals from distant ports. The Council of Ten swore not to reveal its proceedings on penalty of death and dismemberment. Words were spoken, secrets whispered, and masks donned and discarded as if Bigio were not there. He was born into the shadows, and that is where he remained. Schooled by disregard, he observed with an outsider's keen eye and sharply tuned ear the life that swirled about his ignored presence. He was a connoisseur of codes, a reader of gesture and unguarded glances, a listener to silences and words not spoken. A man too much in love with himself did not think others worthy of his attention. Bigio walked the city clear-eyed, unlike others blessed by nature and blinded by their own self-regard.

Secrets came to Bigio free and unbidden. He never betrayed the trust of his sources or the friends and foreigners who showed him hospitality at home and generosity at the café. He never had been a paid spy for the Council, never dropped a note of accusation signed or unsigned into the mouths of the stone lions scattered about the city that swallowed the lives of many malefactors and more than a few innocent men. He never sent a man, guilty or innocent, into exile or to his death in a dank cell in the bowels of the Ducal Palace.

"Find out the truth, Stefano. You see things others don't. People trust you. They know you're an honorable man. Moliterni's widow, you helped her at no benefit to yourself. Remember Strozzi's son."

"That was easy – that wasn't a man buried for four years." Strozzi, a wealthy spice merchant in the parish, came to Zampelli last year worried about the changed behavior of his only son. A few years over twenty, handsome but not taken to foppish ways, he had always been a dutiful son, hardworking, not one to sneak away at night with flimsy stories of his whereabouts the next morning. The father was afraid the boy was embezzling from the family business but didn't confront him for fear of driving him further into the embrace of whatever costly sins now held him. It took Bigio only a week or so, a few questions in the market and café, and a garrulous gondolier, his tongue loosened by too much wine, who broke his guild's code of silence. A patrician's wife, caught in a loveless marriage to a much older man with a taste for beardless boys, was old enough to be his mother but young enough to seduce the merchant's son with her beauty. Seduced or seducer it didn't matter to the young man's father. He was too much a Venetian to be morally offended and was rather proud of his son's amorous adventures. But it was dangerous for a citizen to have an affair above his station. A whispered word from an aggrieved patrician, and father and son might find themselves before the Council Against Blasphemy. The son was quickly shipped off to an uncle in the Levant. The grateful father made a generous donation to San Pantalon's rebuilding. Bigio accepted an unsolicited gift that helped supplement the Republic's meager dole for clothing and food.

"Even if he's a murderer?"

"Fumiani...never."

Bigio didn't hold out much hope for a body buried four years with no questions or tears. Things had of way of disappearing into the mist in Venice, especially if someone wanted them to disappear. "Are you doing this just to get me to mass?"

"I'm just a humble parish priest. I leave the difficult work to God."

Bigio hadn't known Fumiani and didn't care about his reputation. No voice had been raised in four years about the dead man. Why did it matter now? Bigio admired Zampelli's loyalty to a friend, even a dead one. A few years younger than Bigio, Zampelli was the third son of a friend of his father's. His eldest brother was the only one allowed to marry, and, like many young patricians, he entered the Church more to preserve the family fortune than to serve God. Though he was not their parish priest, Zampelli had helped settle several disputes between Bigio's father and his creditors and drew up the wills for Bigio's father and brother. He had served the family well. He was owed Bigio's good efforts. Bigio would try to find out the truth for Zampelli's sake, for the honor of the Bigio name, and even more for the nameless corpse buried beneath the marble floor of San Pantalon. No one should die unknown and unmourned. The dead man deserved a name, and his family, if he had any, deserved to know his fate and say a prayer for his soul.

Zampelli pointed to the space between two windows on the left side of the nave. Four large muscled figures crouched under the painted architecture. "Those grim looking ones, they're Pride and Anger. Those gentler ones, Peace and Justice. Not my body of course, not even when I was in the prime of my youth." The priest smiled, "The face of Justice is my face as Giovanni remembered it from my younger days. Stefano, do this for justice."

Justice was a creature rarely found in Venice. She surely was not blind, not in the Republic. Money and power tipped her scales. As soon as a law was made, an evasion was found. There wasn't a law of God or the Republic that wasn't sidestepped or forgotten for a pocketful of ducats. Any man with a good name, quick wit, and money could slither free from under the heavy cloak of God's commandments and the Republic's laws – first always a Venetian, then a Christian. If a man was murdered and the murderer was a mason or a carpenter, he would end up on the gibbet in San Marco. If the murderer had friends in the Great Council or if he were a patrician with his name registered in the Republic's Golden Book of noble families, he likely would go unpunished. Bigio would leave divine justice to God, if He hadn't already washed his hands of the Venetians. At best, Bigio could only hope to trouble the sleep of the guilty with the knowledge that others knew of their crimes. Then again, the guilty might be dead and buried on the Giudecca.

"Father, you might not like the truth."

"Stefano, God loves the truth."

Fumiani went by the name of Paolo Tiarini on the Giudecca. Only the priest at San Eufemia knew the old man was Fumiani. Bigio told Zampelli to send word to the priest not to tell anyone else. He would go to the Giudecca tomorrow.

"Where can I find Fumiani's widow?

"In heaven. Sweet, beautiful woman died of grief less than a year after Fumiani was buried."

Bigio didn't correct Zampelli. "Didn't she recognize the man buried in the church wasn't her husband?

"She didn't see the body. I thought it would disturb her to see him so mutilated." Zampelli tugged again on his chin. "I did it for her own good. She was a delicate woman. She never bore him any children. She lost a child or two in the womb. She was simply too delicate to bring them into the world."

"Who besides his wife knew Fumiani best?"

Zampelli glanced up at the ceiling. "Saint Pantalon. They were companions for twenty years."

The images painted on the walls and ceilings of the city's churches were stories for the unlettered, some more colorful than others. Bigio paid them only passing attention. The martyred saint was a mute witness who could tell him nothing.

"Someone among the living, Father."

"I think the widow's father is still alive. He has an apothecary, the Angel, in Campo San Bartolomeo."

Bigio planted the tip of his walking stick on the marble floor and pushed himself up from the bench.

"Stefano, are you eating well?"

"Well enough." Bigio learned to think on an empty stomach and turn a deaf ear to its rumbling.

"And that Muslim drink?" Zampelli smiled.

"My only vice. But only if it is worth drinking."

Zampelli pulled a stained pouch from beneath his cassock and took out a few coins. "For some good coffee."

Bigio didn't ask for the money, so he took it without shame. He wouldn't use it to buy information – that was what a spy did. He might buy conversation over a cup of coffee or a glass of wine. Maybe there would be a few coins left over.

Zampelli motioned for him to sit. "Stay a while longer. Light a candle, ask for Saint Pantalon's help."

5

One of the Fourteen Holy Helpers, healer of body and soul, the all-compassionate Saint Pantalon, the son of a wealthy pagan in Nicomedia, was instructed in the Christian faith by his mother Saint Eubula. Physician to the Emperor Maximian, he was besieged daily in the idolatrous court by the false wisdom of the world and fell into apostasy. Sainted Hermolaus, the bishop of the city, brought him back into the faith. What use were the medical arts, Hermolaus asked, when you are ignorant of the science of salvation, and who, he wanted to know, was a better physician than Christ? Pantalon gave a blind man back his sight by calling upon the name of Christ. This miracle converted Pantalon's father, who at his death bequeathed his fortune to his son. Pantalon freed his many slaves and gave his wealth away to the poor of the city. Pagan doctors jealous of his reputation for goodness denounced him to the emperor who urged him to renounce his faith once again. Pantalon refused, embraced his faith openly, and showed the power of Christ as the true and only God by healing a paralytic before the emperor's eyes. Pantalon's evil-tongued colleagues told the emperor it was no miracle, only a conjurer's cheap trick, and the emperor condemned Pantalon to death for his faith.

Burned with torches, Christ extinguished the flames. Cast into a cauldron of molten lead, Christ cooled the bubbling inferno. Weighted with a great stone and hurled into the sea, Christ turned the stone light as a feather. Thrown into a pit of wild beasts, the animals turned docile as lambs. Bound to a wheel and sent down a rocky slope, the ropes snapped and the wheel broke. And when Pantalon's neck was laid beneath the executioner's sword, Christ bent the executioner's blade. His executioners fell to their knees converted by Christ's miraculous protection and were forgiven by the merciful Pantalon. Only when Pantalon welcomed death did the blade slice through his neck. The olive tree to which he was bound fruited from the milk and blood that flowed from his severed neck.

Bigio looked up at Emperor Maximian, bare-chested and haughty, sitting in a courtyard surrounded by six court physicians near the top of terraced steps steep as a mountain cliff. Some crouched beneath the emperor, others leaned over his shoulders, all whispered denunciations of their fellow healer. Not because Pantalon had turned his back on the pagan gods and returned to the Christian faith of his dead mother. No such honorable motives. They were not thinking of their gods but their purses. They envied Pantalon's inherited wealth that he gave away to the poor and resented his reputation for healing the blind and infirm. They acted out of petty self-interest not principle. Bigio thought them no different from the patricians who huddled in the Broglio offering their votes to the highest bidder or conniving to advance their own ambitions.

Bigio's neck ached. He looked down at the tips of his worn boots. After a few moments, he looked up again at the torturers with their instruments of cruelty, the executioners, the hooded pagan priests urging Pantalon to renounce his faith, the pagan spectators killed by flying pieces of the broken wheel, and the swirling angels, seen from below, floating in the golden light of heaven as Pantalon with arms extended rose to meet his Savior. What men with more learned eyes than his said was true: there was no ceiling in Venice that matched its scale, its dizzying illusion, its obvious ambition. The many canvases did not simply cover the ceiling but curved downward to the walls of the church between the large windows high up on either side of the nave. An angel above the altar, legs extended into space, spread his wings ready to take flight from the ceiling itself. The solid columns of the church extended upward into the painted colonnades and arcades of the painted cupola and courtyard that opened into the infinity of heaven. It was to Bigio a wondrous work. Why would a man flee his life at the height of his career while praise swirled about him like the angels in heaven?

6

The gondola sliced across the Giudecca Canal toward San Eufemia. A light spray driven by the wind moistened Bigio's cheeks. He didn't wear a mask though the law allowed impoverished patricians to hide their shame even when Carnival had passed. A mask got in the way. With narrow ellipses cut for the eyes, he could only see straight ahead. In Venice the truth lay at the margins, not in the obvious mummery of processions and pageantry. Banished to the margins by fate, Bigio paid attention to what went on in the corners and edges of life.

Bigio had not been to the Giudecca for years, not even for the Feast of the Redentore. When he was a child, his father, who thought it better to drown in a big sea than float in shallow water, spared no expense to celebrate the Feast. While crowds walked across to the Giudecca on a temporary bridge of barges stretched across the canal, his father in prodigal extravagance hired a flotilla of flower-festooned boats to bring family and friends over to celebrate under summer stars until the dawn. Bigio's greasy fingers tingled from the heat of fried sole bought fresh from a hawker's booth. He watched acrobats somersault through the air in front of houses and shops hung with garlands of flowers, flags, and tapestries woven with mythic adventures and Venetian victories. Fortunetellers surrounded by crystal spheres and polished globes whispered his future – when he had one – into a tin tube to make it sound glorious and ordained.

Other memories of the Giudecca were not as pleasant. It was

over fifty years ago in a candle-lit ballroom at a patrician's sum-
merhouse. Though he couldn't remember her name, Bigio could
still see her face and the sprig of pomegranate tucked behind her
ear. She didn't know his virginal infatuation. She was too young
and callow to understand the pain she caused. She thought it a
harmless joke, if she gave it any thought at all. A cripple, like a
court dwarf or a blackamoor, was an amusement for the beautiful
and well formed. Candles were snuffed out for the *torcia* and the
music began. She held a torch above her head like a Greek goddess.
She circled the darkened room to find her handsome favorite. She
passed Bigio without a glance. She curtsied before her chosen and
signaled for Bigio to take the torch to light their way. The couple
glided around the room. He shuffled beside them burning with
humiliation beneath the flickering flame.

Patricians fallen on hard times came to the Giudecca in summer
as guests to walk in gardens fragrant with the perfume of orange
and citron trees, enjoy cool evening breezes, and listen to the
sweet voices of the orphan girls brought from the Ospedale della
Pieta. Like the innocents of that angel choir, poor patricians were
expected to sing for their supper. Bigio would rather swelter and
starve in his room than be a court jester kept around to amuse with
buffoonish banter.

The gondolier helped Bigio step ashore in front of San Eufemia.
A large gray rat scrambled up the wet stairs, turned his head, and
looked at him before scurrying across the stones and disappearing
behind a low pyramid of barrels. "Brother rat, sorry to disturb your
day, I won't be long," Bigio said softly under his breath. He walked
into the dimly lit church to meet the priest who was to take him to
Fumiani's room. The priest, tall and gaunt like a stylite down from
his pillar, looked to be as old as Zampelli and had a broad toothy
smile that seemed an odd match to his ascetic appearance.

"I have known Zampelli since we were boys...since he was as
thin as I am," the priest said. "I saw Fumiani up on the scaffold
several times. Staring at the canvas, adding touches. Changing

things. Always making changes. It looked beautiful to me, but I guess not to him. Zampelli would call up, 'Come down, only God can make a heaven more beautiful.' 'Not yet' he'd say and wave us away and turn back to his painting. I remembered the way he stared down at us. When I saw the drawings in his room, it struck me."

"You didn't suspect before?"

"I only spoke to him a few times. Fumiani was dead. What was there to suspect?"

Fumiani arrived on the Giudecca three years before but rarely came to San Eufemia. He kept to himself. The priest rarely saw him walking along the canal in the early evening or fishing for squid at the edge of the canal under the moonlight like many men and boys on the Giudecca did. He said he was a widower from Padua where he had worked at the Botanical Gardens. On the Giudecca he picked up work in some of the palazzo gardens in spring and summer and helped tend the flowers at Le Zitelle. The nuns at the church who gave shelter to young maidens without dowries preferred old men working in the garden. There was little danger an old man would capture the hearts of the poor, young girls or seduce them to sell their virtue in the brothels of Castelletto.

"Did he come to confession very often?"

The priest smiled as if Bigio were a naughty child who should have known better.

"Well, if he did come to confession, what do you think he might have said?"

"Father, I have sinned."

Now it was Bigio's turn to smile. "We all have."

They walked out of the church and along the canal. The dark water lapped against the pilings. Gulls stood silent sentinels atop the rotting wood. "Old men like you and me reminisce," the priest said. "We chew old memories like tough meat. This fellow didn't. He didn't seem like a man who wanted to talk about the past."

The priest turned at the first corner, stopped, and waited for

Bigio to catch up. "Once I saw him coming down the stairs of Redentore. That's a long walk. Why go all the way to the other end of the Giudecca I asked, when you could turn the corner and be at the altar of San Eufemia without having to catch your breath. He smiled and said he liked the walk. Said he liked the view across the canal. I don't think that was the reason. He just said that to end the conversation. There must have been something else. Maybe he wanted to look back and remember his old life."

7

Bigio expected disorder and the lingering stench of death. Instead he found a room neat and ordered as a monk's cell. The landlord assured him he hadn't touched a thing. The priest told him not to, and anyway it was bad luck.

Along one wall was a narrow bed, sheet pulled taut, smooth as marble, and a rough gray wool blanket across the foot of the bed, folded in a neat rectangle. Three small brushes, two quill and two reed pens, four pencils and a half dozen pieces of dark chalk lay side by side like soldiers on parade along the top of a long ink-stained table pushed against the opposite wall. Small bottles of brown and black ink nudged each other on a narrow wooden tray. Several dozen sheets of paper lay stacked neatly at the corner of the table. Bigio leafed through the sheets, careful to keep them in the order he found them. Angels and putti seen from below floated in space. A delicate hand pointed right, another pointed left, a soft arm reached upward. The curly haired heads of angels and putti covered one sheet. With a few simple sharp black lines Fumiani drew the wings and soles of angels and the smooth round bellies of putti. On several sheets, swords, shields, and swags of fruit and flowers drawn in pencil and chalk were brushed with a light wash of ink. The sheets were full of light and shadow. A single female head filled one sheet, her hair a luxuriant halo of lines and shading. Her gentleness and beatific calm made Bigio think her the Virgin Mary. As if pulled by some invisible thread, he touched her cheek with the tips of his fingers before putting the sheet back on the pile.

"There's more," the landlord said, pointing to a cheap oak chest at the foot of the bed. In the small chest five thick journals bound in heavy rough brown paper sat atop a stained jacket, some rough cotton shirts, and a few other odd pieces of well-worn clothes. Bigio took out the top journal and sat on the edge of the chest, not wanting to disturb the dead man's well-made bed. He flicked quickly through the curled pages, most filled with geometric shapes, angles of various degrees, scribbled figures and equations, columns plain and fluted, pedestals, cornices, and other architectural elements Bigio couldn't name. A hand, a foot, a curly head of hair, the curve of a neck were all drawn with a quick, light stroke as if Fumiani were thinking out loud with quill and pen, as if he were afraid to lift pen from paper for fear the image in his mind would disappear. The landlord said these were all that they found. Bigio turned the journal over and put it back atop the other four. Bigio asked the landlord to have the chest sent to him so he could look more carefully through the journals.

The gardens of Le Zitelle were hidden behind a high stone wall. Bigio smelled the fragrance of unseen orange and lemon trees. Looking through two wrought iron gates spaced along the wall, he saw sections of the herb gardens, canopies of roses at one end, and ivy blanketing a far brick wall. He imagined Fumiani on his knees, tending to the basil and oregano plants, his fingertips and nails, once rainbowed with reds and blues, now dark with dirt. Fumiani swept the herringbone brick path clear of fallen rose petals, bent down, and picked up a red petal and held it above his head. Sunlight turned it an almost luminous pink like the cloak of the winged angel soaring above the altar of San Pantalon. He stood entranced by the glowing petal. After a moment or two he shook himself free from the petal's spell and continued his sweeping.

Bigio made his way back to the Fondamenta Sant'Eufemia. The wind had picked up, and the canal was choppy. Clouds scudded across the sky. He waited for an approaching gondola. He imagined Fumiani standing on the water's edge looking across the Giudecca Canal at his past life like an exile looking down from a winding mountain path on the city he had left and could never enter again. Bigio understood that feeling of loss for he himself often looked across the Grand Canal at the palazzo where he was born and from which he had been banished.

Perhaps there were times Fumiani risked his new life and travelled across the canal. Cloak wrapped tight around his shoulders, a cowl obscuring his face, he went when the fog hung thickly over the lagoon to disappear unnoticed into his past. He glided like an invisible specter through familiar streets and piazzas, past shopkeepers he would have greeted in his old life with a wave, a smile, or a few words. An advantage of being dead was people didn't expect to see him. Certain of his death, they doubted their senses. They saw what they expected to see. Especially when he didn't acknowledge their stares, with even a fleeting gaze. Fumiani and he might have brushed shoulders in San Marco, begged each other's pardon, and gone their separate ways. Fumiani was close as a hand's touch from his old life and yet as far away as a merchant sailing off the coast of Cathay. Maybe learning of his wife's death, he went to San Pantalon to light a candle for her soul in Purgatory, if God in his unfathomable mystery hadn't already welcomed her to heaven. In the dim chapel Fumiani looked at Veronese's Saint Pantalon and the ill child the saint cured with God's grace. He lit another candle. Fumiani the painter was dead. Tiarini the gardener said a prayer for the painter's soul, not yet departed, but surely headed for Purgatory.

8

The butcher's son lugged Fumiani's chest from the Giudecca to Bigio's room with the help of friendly gondolier. The boy was a wiry lad of fourteen or fifteen whose eager disposition wasn't dampened by the purple birthmark that stained his left cheek like a pool of spilled ink. He liked the old man who drew pictures of him in payment, along with a few coins, for going to an apothecary near I Frari to buy paper and chalk. "He painted my good side," the boy said, slapping his right cheek playfully. "He was one particular fellow. Wrote out the kind of paper and chalk he wanted. He'd stand at the window and hold the sheets up to the light and run his fingers gently across the paper as if it were a baby's soft crown. He knew as much about paper and chalk as my father does about butchering a pig. I told him he should paint a church, but he just shook his head and said he was an ordinary gardener and no artist at all. Look at those angels, he had a gift."

"Why didn't the old man go to buy the materials himself?"

"He said he was just a humble gardener and didn't feel welcome in a fancy place where great artists came to buy their paints and ink."

Bigio fished in the bottom of his leather pouch for a few coins from Zampelli's offering and paid the boy for his trouble. Bigio was in no rush to look at the drawings. He was more comfortable in the company of words. He understood words, paid attention to them. The armor that stood gleaming in the *portego* of the family palazzo, its terrazzo floor buffed and polished till it shone like a mirror, was his favorite as a child, more appealing than the somber paintings of long dead ancestors and saints on the walls. Martyred saints and winged angels were everywhere in Venice. He took their presence for granted, like the gondolas that crisscrossed the canals and the seagulls that floated above the dark water. Bigio admired the courage of martyrs but not the priests, who seemed to take pleasure in marking their suffering, torture by bloody torture, pain by piercing pain. His fellow Venetians may have longed for salvation, but they found it too serene and boring for their flawed natures, preferring the drama of suffering. The handiwork of artists who conjured up fanciful images of saintly suffering and heavenly reward might be necessary instruction in the faith for the unlettered. For Bigio the painted figures and tales, however bright and bold, couldn't express the faceted truths that words revealed.

Bigio swept his hand toward the opened chest. "Jude, look what I have for you. Lovely paper to line your cage." Bigio didn't think there were any clues to mine from Fumiani's journals or the sheets of floating figures. Fumiani's angels seemed well drawn, but he couldn't tell if they were ascending to heaven or tumbling to earth. Even if Fumiani left behind journals full of his thoughts, could anyone understand the contours of another man's soul? We lived in a world of strangers, Bigio thought, even those we called by their first name and whose lives we believed were a mirror of our own. The masks people wore kept their true selves hidden from others. Even from themselves. Some wore them so long and so well that the masks became their true selves. Even God sometimes was baffled. He pulled on his long white beard, scratched his divine head, and wondered, "What have I done? Who are these people?"

9

It was Thursday, his day. Bigio sat in the small ground floor parlor, waiting to be summoned to Carla Franco's bedroom. Her young maid took one step into the parlor and tugged at the front of her faded brown frock. Once Carla had a houseboy and two maids. Now she was down to a slow moving, thick-waisted girl from Pellestrina with village manners.

"My mistress will see you in a few minutes. She's drying her hair." the maid said.

When Carla was younger, she sat on the wooden loggia overlooking the campo beneath the rose entwined trellis and chatted with Bigio as she bleached her hair under the late afternoon sun. She wore a silk cape over her shoulders and a broad brimmed straw hat with the top cut off. Her thick hair, wet with a secret potion, haloed over the brim, turning gold as corn silk in the sunlight. Now self-conscious about her thinning hair, she bleached her hair alone.

Her maid didn't have to lead Bigio upstairs – he knew the way. Forty-five years of Thursdays – that had been and was his day. The other days had been taken by men equally under her thrall. Now all were empty except for Thursday and Wednesday, long reserved for a retired admiral who, when his gout didn't flare up, clung to the habit of her company. All the rest of Carla Franco's lovers were dead. Except for Wednesday, Bigio could visit Carla any day he wanted, but for her sake he kept up the charade of a life full of besotted lovers.

Bigio had never spoken to Admiral Moroni. He saw him only at a distance in the Great Council. He was a stout, short man, with a stentorian voice and imposing presence. When he spoke in the Great Council, not a spit was heard. Bigio purposely avoided the man. He didn't want to hear him talk of Carla. He didn't want to think of him in her bed, her soft flesh touched by his arthritic fingers. One of the heroes of the Morean War, he likely spoke to her only of himself and his past accomplishments, uninterested in the lives and opinions of others. Carla true to a courtesan's discretion never spoke of him. Bigio thought perhaps she would break the code of her calling if he said anything witty or of importance on current matters of significance to the Republic. He was likely a boring man stuck in the past tolerated by Carla out of sympathy for the vigorous man he once was. Bigio admitted to himself and Jude that he was jealous of the man. Bigio wanted to have Carla to himself only.

Carla's age was a mystery. Bigio thought she was a few years older than he, which would have made her over seventy. Her fine features had not coarsened, her flesh not grown ample and flaccid. By some miracle, perhaps it was the humid sea air, balm from the Levant, or a secretion from a rare feline in the jungles of Cathay, her cheeks retained the alabaster smoothness of a young woman. She moved with a sweet and facile grace when young. Now she walked deliberately, slightly bent over. Yet there was still about her the gamin's charm. When younger she wore men's trousers under her skirts – it was then the fashion among courtesans – and played the smooth-cheeked boy if that was her lover's fancy. A bishop from Padua, a regular visitor long gone to the company of saints, was rumored to have taken the back door with her. That wasn't Bigio's taste.

Every visit there was a moment when Carla turned towards him and was once again the twenty-year-old courtesan that brought men of wealth and power from the capitals of Europe to Venice, an attraction no less renowned than the Titians of I

Frari and the mosaics of San Marco. In that singular moment his heart shuddered, as it did the first time her silk chemise fell from her shoulders and he saw her naked breasts. He remembered the sweet good fortune of their youthful evenings together and how the disappointments of the world disappeared in the refuge of her perfumed bed. He saw her faint smile and knew she too remembered the effect she had on him. The faint scent of jasmine summoned distant evenings when he came early to find her lounging in her scented bath. He undressed quickly and sat opposite her in the warm water. Their fingers traced soft ribbons on each other's thighs and touched their sexes beneath the water until his passion couldn't be contained. They rose hand in hand from the bath, embraced, and tumbled together onto the bed. She sat astride him, beads of water dripping from her breasts onto his chest.

Her spotted and arthritic hands betrayed her age. She wore lace gloves indoors and out. When Bigio crossed his legs, she pointed out a small hole in his stockings – the same one as the week before – and told him to wear another his next visit so she could darn this pair. They both knew it was an empty offer. Her fingers couldn't handle needle and thread, and anyway this was his best pair.

Carla lived on the dwindling inheritance of lovers long buried. They were patricians of some importance who had protected her from the Republic's laws that prohibited courtesans from possessing tapestries, painted chests, silk curtains, and other domestic luxuries, all of which now were worn and shabby. The fine linen atop her dressing table, lined with empty perfume bottles of Murano glass, was long yellowed, the edges of its lace trim frayed to dangling threads. She refused to sell her ivory combs, gilt brushes, gold tweezers, and the tarnished silver-framed mirror. They must, Bigio thought, hold the reflections of her youth. She made Bigio promise that he would make sure she didn't end her days begging for bread or selling candles in church like desperate courtesans reduced to rags and borrower's wine. Bigio was a man of honor. He had no honorable idea of how he would keep his word, but he would.

Bigio knew there had been others, and yet she made him believe that she longed in solitude for the days to speed by until Thursday came again. In those distant nights when he lay inside her it felt as if they were one body. Spent and overwhelmed, he slid his head from cheek to pillow so she couldn't feel his tears of pleasure. Now there were some days they scarcely touched. Her fingers grazed his cheek, his hand lay on her breast, and he felt her sparrow's heart beating. Her head rested on his chest, she recited love sonnets of Petrarch, and lying on the bed's faded coverlet they drifted toward slumber. Some nights they lay next to each other, hip to hip, hands crisscrossed lightly on each other's thighs like virginal youths. Carla never stayed in bed when Bigio left, not even when they were younger and their energetic lovemaking left her floating on the edge of sleep. Not to get up and show him out of her bedroom would signal that the pleasures she offered were only carnal, that she was no better than a common prostitute in the Castelletto.

He believed, though she wouldn't admit it, that she would have welcomed him even if he couldn't pay for her one day's company. She too looked forward to Thursday. In his arms she was still the corsair of Venus sought after by patricians and foreigners of wealth and taste. Bound by time and affection they were more than courtesan and client.

Carla sat on a small, brocaded settee, her head turned to show what she thought was her best side. Her gloved hand rested lightly on a single strand of pearls that Bigio gave her when he was young, his father was still alive, and Bigio had money to spare. She wore the necklace whenever Bigio visited, though courtesans were forbidden to wear pearls even indoors. Across from the settee was her bed with its gilded posts in need of retouching and tatty purple curtains. Bigio smelled the faint scent of musk and a whisper of garlic from the kitchen below. She patted the cushion next to her with a gloved hand.

Bigio held out his hand, a small red stone gleamed in his palm. "A ruby for me?"

"Only you."

Smiling, she took the gem and put it atop many other companions gleaming red, blue, and deep green in a small alabaster bowl in the middle of the small round marble top table next to the settee. It was a game they had long played.

When Bigio was nine his father entrusted him with a narrow rectangular box about a foot long and four inches high made of a dark, reddish wood whose grain looked like steep peaked mountains to his young eyes. The box, his father said, was from China and was filled with sapphires, rubies, and emeralds from the mines of India. His father came to his room every week or so and take a jewel "to turn to gold." One night Bigio overheard his mother berating his father for his prodigal habits that would leave the family in rags. Bigio told his brother that he was going to give all the jewels back to his father and save the family. Gregorio, precocious and less protected than his lame older brother, took a ruby from the box and threw it down on the marble floor, shattering the gem into a shower of glittering red slivers. Now less than two-dozen Murano glass gems, for that is what they were, remained in the warped and cracked box. Bigio carried two or three in his pocket, rubbing them between his fingers like Greek merchants with their worry beads, to remind him of the cheap glass that lay beneath the glittering surface of the world.

The maid brought Bigio a cup of coffee on a tarnished salver. He took one sip and put the cup down on the table. The coffee had been brewed in the morning and sat all day before she reheated it.

"I have come from church to see you."

"My dear Stefano, why after all these years must you lie? You would no more go to church on Thursday than be caught drinking cheap Greek wine in a *malvasie*."

"To see you, my Holy Virgin, my blessed Mary Magdalene."

She smiled, and her eyes came alive. She had been a favorite of the city's painters with her unblemished skin and innocent gaze that belied all she saw of man's hidden demons and lustful obsessions.

41

In many Venetian churches she knelt forever young, hand on heart, eyes looking upward at the angel Gabriel floating before her. In the flickering candlelight of side chapels she held the infant Jesus in all his blessed plumpness. Jealous women, who spoke ill of her kind and the lives they led, knelt in prayer before her Mary Magdalene slumped in grief at the foot of the cross. Bigio lit many candles over the years at the altar of her gaze and her radiant flesh when Thursday seemed far off.

"Who was the first to paint you?"

"The first one? You always remember your first one," she put her cup down to free her hand for the telling. "I was seventeen. My friend posed for him and told me he was a naughty man – that was why he was called the Libertine. He made me wear a robe of silk so fine you could see the hairs of my mound. I already was well known. My nights were all taken. I was sure he asked me to be his model just to get me into his bed. He wanted for free what others fought to pay for. But…" she paused, "he is a sweet man…"

He isn't a sweet man, he *was* a sweet man, but Bigio had given up correcting her when she spoke of lovers long dead, as if they walked the stones of the city.

"He just painted me." She laid her hand on Bigio's knee. "He paid me more to keep my clothes on than most men paid me to take them off. He never touched me except to push a strand or two of hair from my forehead and bunch the fabric of my dress so he could see how the folds of cloth looked in the sunlight. The first time, he sat me in a chair and had me lean my head against the wall. You're a saint, he said, you're having a vision. I didn't move. My body ached, my stomach growled. It seemed like hours. I'm having a vision, I said. The Angel Gabriel? he asked. No, a plate of shrimp and a glass of wine. My little shrimp, he called me, just another minute or two. From then on whenever I posed for him, there was always a plate of shrimp and a bottle of wine for me."

"Did Fumiani ever paint you?"

"There were so many, I can't remember them all. Fumiani…the

poor fellow who fell off the scaffold? I don't think so. I did see him a few weeks before he died. Why the sudden interest? I've tried to make you a more cultured gentleman, Stefano, but without success. You've never been one to speak of art."

"Zampelli, the priest at San Pantalon, has asked me to handle some parish affairs. Unpaid bills you could say." Bigio knew Carla well enough to know she didn't believe him and in time would learn the truth. She read the tone of his voice, the words he spoke, his hesitations, his silences. After all their years, there was nothing he could hide from her.

"I went to see the ceiling. Well not really, I went to see the Electress of Bavaria. I heard she was a beauty. She was. The young daughter of the Polish king, you know. I still remember her lovely dress. The color of honey, brocaded with pearls and emeralds. The sleeves were pinched with ruby clasps. And her fingers, I remember her fingers. The slimmest, longest fingers I ever saw."

Bigio wanted to know what she thought of the painting. "So many people. You know it isn't a very big church. We were packed in like salted fish in a barrel. I barely had room to lean my head back and look up. It hurt my neck to look. I didn't see very much. It seemed finished to me. I should go back, shouldn't I?"

"What do you mean finished?"

"Don't you remember? All the talk of how he insulted the Electress. It was in the *Gazzetta*. He said it wasn't finished. He didn't want to uncover it, even if it was only for a week. The Electress heard word about this magnificent painting that covered the entire ceiling. She had to see it while she was here. Word came down from the doge himself. It would serve the interests of the Republic if the wife of the Elector of Bavaria saw it. What could he do? He couldn't say no. I caught a glimpse of him walking by her side, pointing up at the ceiling. I couldn't hear what he was telling her. With all that praise and attention, you would have thought him a happy man. But he didn't look happy – I have an eye for unhappy men." She paused to summon up the memory. "He was wearing a smock, all stained with paint. To meet royalty, you would have thought he would have taken it off. Wearing that dirty smock was an insult, don't you think? A few weeks later he fell." She turned away. Saddened by her memories, she looked down at her worn fur-lined slippers.

Fumiani rose in Bigio's eyes for wearing a dirty smock. It wasn't intended as an insult. This was what he wore when he worked on his art. It was a mark of respect, the most worthy garment to honor a lady of such high rank who wanted to see his work. Wearing his smock was just his way of telling the people at the Palace the painting wasn't finished. Did the doge think he was a simple mechanical? Would a mason let people walk across a bridge whose stones were not set?

The light was fading. Carla rang a small crystal bell to summon her maid, whom Bigio was sure was hovering in the hall eavesdropping on her mistress. The maid lit candles on the dressing table and on the table next to the bed. The room seemed even dimmer in the sad, flickering light. When they were younger, this might be the time when Carla played the lute. Now she hid her bent fingers beneath lace gloves, and the lute lay warped and cracked in the painted cassone at the foot of the bed. In their shared silence Bigio imagined Carla watching a body tumble from the scaffolding high above the nave, arms wildly reaching for the ankles of painted angels and grasping only air. She grieved for an artist at the threshold of his success, while Bigio wondered what Fumiani told the young princess, who had commanded him to do what he didn't want to do.

10

"A bill collector, Stefano? Don't do anything that brings dishonor to your name."

"It's an honest job. Debts should be paid."

Carla knew Bigio well. He was, she said, the last of a dying breed, a man who said "no" to the easy opportunity. Under the Republic's laws a patrician couldn't dirty his hands with a crafts-man's tool or soil his soul behind a shop counter. Many a poor patrician – no more than a silk clad beggar – turned to intrigue and immorality to fill their idle days and empty purses. There were things Bigio pledged he would never do. He was approached many times to sell his vote in the Great Council, but he never had and wouldn't, however many other patricians did, however worn his patrician's toga or empty his purse. Let other poor patricians barter their honor in front of the Ducal Palace like Swiss mercenaries. He wouldn't pass off the toenail clippings of a fishmonger's wife as the sacred remains of Saint Ursula or claim a small beaker of goat's milk was the sacred breast milk of the Holy Virgin herself. If a foreigner was lost in the city's maze at night, he guided them to safety. If a lady needed a hand in getting out of a gondola, or if he could stand aside to give the faithful a better view of a venerated image or a glimpse of the doge himself and not just the top of his golden parasol as a procession passed by, he accepted with feigned reluctance a modest tip for what were simply good manners. If a foreign visitor asked, he offered a word or two on the city's most favored courtesans and where they could be found and didn't refuse a few coins for the information. These were true services, needed and done with honest intent. No one was misled, cheated, or suffered an indignity by his actions.

Bigio didn't have income from investments or land and couldn't afford the servants, fine clothing, and entertainment that important state offices required. The positions he could afford were demeaning sinecures beneath his name and pride. It would have shamed him into an early grave to sit behind a desk earning a mean fee from replacements he recruited for office holders absent from their duties. Nature's curse made a military commission out of the question. Even if he had been born with two good legs, he didn't like the idea of killing a man he didn't know personally. Many patrician families tottering on the abyss of destitution sent their sons, no matter their spiritual fitness, into the church. Everyone sinned, everyone was fallen, but Bigio had no tolerance for priests who loved flesh more than God and fathered a brood of bastards or serviced nuns in a convent like whores in a brothel. He forgave them their lust, not their hypocrisy.

Patricians, what a devalued coin they now were. Fine wine turned to vinegar. Carla called him a cynic, but he was a clear-eyed realist, who saw the slow creeping death in the clouded eyes of the Republic. Venice had become a floating cabinet of curiosities for gawking Englishmen. Carla heard his complaints before. Bigio kept his tongue today. He didn't want to be one of these café bores yapping and wagging his finger at the fallen world. The Bigios had been in the Golden Book since the fourteenth century along with the Valieros, the Querinis, the Morosinis, and other families of renown and great service to the Republic, not like the new nobility who bought their way into the register. The Republic, its coffers emptied by war and folly, was selling its soul. The Widmanns were once street porters, the Castelli, drapers, the Fonsecas, sellers of sugar, and the Zolios, bloodstained pork butchers. They tried hard to hide their recent past, but you could smell the stink of the market stall under their ermine cloaks.

"Be careful. Some people don't want to pay their bills."

"If I end up dead in some dark alley, no one is going to throw themselves in the canal out of grief. No one will think the bottom has dropped out of their life."

"I will. But only on Thursday," Carla laughed.

Bigio knew better. If he was found floating in a canal or fell to his death from a shaky scaffold, Carla would hurry to see him one last time, though his body was broken and his face a gruesome mask. No priest would stop her. Bigio couldn't imagine that a woman who loved a man wouldn't fight to see his body one last time. Even if it were only to rub the sleeve of his shirt between her fingers or gently touch his cheek and hand, the hand that had picked up pen and brush to the praise of many, the hand that had given her a good life.

Carla took his hand in hers. Her voice was soft, "My dear Stefano, I would rather be your lover than the doge's wife."

They lay atop the coverlet. He softly ran his finger along her lips. She leaned her head back, inviting him to kiss her on the neck. He drew soft circles on her breasts and felt her nipples turn firm to the touch of his fingers and lips. He kissed her nipples. They kissed gently opened mouthed, breathing air one into the other to save themselves from drowning. She lay her cheek on his beating heart, her arm across his stomach. He put his arm round her bare shoulders. Neither wanted to move, to break the bond of flesh and feeling. This was all they wanted today. It was enough.

As Bigio was about to leave, the maid called from the top of the stairs for him to wait. She trudged down the stairs as if walking through thick mud. "Mistress Carla remembers. Anna Ridolfi, an old acquaintance of hers, was a companion," she said the word with a sly smile, "of the man you are interested in. She thinks she lives near the Campo San Polo...if she hasn't given up her soul to God her master."

11

The fruit monger in Campo San Margherita put four figs in the straw basket at the feet of a white-haired woman. While she slowly counted out her coins, he sneaked an extra two figs into the basket. The fruit monger's wife, a stout dark-haired woman visibly pregnant, wiped her hands on her white apron streaked purple from plums. She clicked her tongue and shook her head as the old woman shuffled away across the campo stones.

"You will make a beggar of us all," she said with exasperated resignation. Her husband pretended not to hear. This was a domestic drama Bigio witnessed often.

The crates at Pietro Acconci's stall were nearly empty. Most of the residents of the campo had finished their morning shopping and were at home preparing the midday meal. Pietro held up two peaches for Bigio to see. He titled his head in the direction of his young daughter, a child of ten, who was helping her mother stack the empty crates.

"Master Bigio, she is a pearl. I wanted a son, but God blessed me with this daughter. She's a lively one, full of ginger. But I tell you master Bigio, I light a candle every day that the next one is a son. If God's deaf, I won't have a moment of silence with three women pestering me day and night." He motioned for his daughter. "Maria and I saved these for you. We know how particular you are. They would wet your beard if you had one." His daughter smiled at Bigio. She was a lovely child with a perpetual smile and bright eyes whose cheeks he had patted and whose blond curls he tousled ever since she began toddling about the stalls doing her best to help her father and mother. She was the niece his sister-in-law denied him.

Bigio knew the peaches were from yesterday or what was left after the better ones were picked over in the morning. He rustled his hand in the empty pocket of his cloak.

"We'll settle up later," Pietro said.

There would be no "later." It was a charade they had played for years, Pietro's generosity increasing as Bigio's cloak grew more faded and worn. Bigio thanked him as he did every morning. Pietro was a wiry fellow, an inch or so shorter than Bigio, with a constant grin, thick, bushy eyebrows arched over mischievous eyes, and, though a good twenty years younger than Bigio, a full head of white hair unkempt as matted straw. Few people in the campo could remember when Pietro's hair wasn't white. He claimed his hair had always been white, a sign that his head was full of pure thoughts.

Pietro had a soft heart for the infirm and the elderly. Bigio was doubly deserving of generosity in Pietro's eyes. Whenever the baker's son pulled his young sister with her shriveled, useless legs through the campo in a small wagon, Pietro waved them over for a handful of grapes or plums wrapped in brown paper. Children who kept their hands by their sides often got a few grapes in exchange for their honesty.

His good cheer, constant chatter, and disheveled appearance made some think him a simple man, his head empty as a dried gourd. Bigio knew better. Not all the spies and informers for the Council of Ten that trawled the city were patricians fallen on hard times or clever and cultivated men who read Ovid and Plutarch in the Latin. There was no shortage of men with open ears and light purses who wanted to be useful to the Republic and earn a spare coin or two in the bargain. No habit or fleeting conversation was too incidental to report to the Council. Spies lounged at apothecaries where gossip along with medicine and pigment passed back and forth across polished counters. They loitered at Carla's door when her days and nights were full, watching the comings and goings of foreigners and faithful patricians. They knew what a man of interest took in his coffee, whom he greeted on his way to the fish market for fresh mullets, which prostitute he favored, and what pleasures he paid extra for. Spies wrote their reports while other spies observed them from the shadows. Gossip and scandal were the favorite fare of cafés, and gondoliers knew more of broken vows and flesh's failings than an elderly priest in the confessional.

Rumor in the campo was that Pietro, with a clean conscience, was sometimes of service to the Council. Who better than a friendly fruit monger in a busy campo to keep his ears and eyes open for a seditious word or suspicious act? Who better to pass on the overheard conversations of a loose-tongued maid in service to a foreigner? He was in the right place to hear whispers about family squabbles, late night liaisons, and a wayward wife carrying another man's child long before the cuckolded husband mistakenly celebrated his good fortune. If the Council offered him money for what he overheard, it would be unpatriotic to refuse its generosity. He asked a question or two to help Bigio with the Strozzi affair and on occasion was a willing ally when a campo neighbor asked the patrician to sift truth from rumor. What he did for the Council was between him and God.

Pietro ran his hands sticky with peach juice through his thick hair. He wrapped a large bunch of grapes in a cone of rough brown paper and handed them to Bigio. "I've had a good day. Here, try these. Sweet as honey. They'd bring a dead man back to life." Pietro smiled and clapped Bigio on the shoulder.

Was it just an ordinary act of generosity and some casual words, or did Pietro know what Father Zampelli had asked Bigio to do? Was he offering his help or warning him that the authorities already knew of the investigation? In time he would answer these questions by something he said or did. Right now, Bigio didn't want to involve his friend in what might turn out to be murder. Bigio pulled a grape loose from the stem and put it in his mouth. A grape or two might be given away, but little else in the city was free. Everything in Venice came with a price.

"Very sweet, but not that sweet."

12

Bigio placed the squashed water bug on the bottom of Saint Jude's cage. "A feast my friend." The sparrow sat unmoving on his perch. "You're right, in this city of secrets the safest path to take is to stay quietly in one's room. I can tell by your sullen silence you want to know why I am troubling with all this, what you call, snooping around. I promised Zampelli, and a man has to keep his promise. But more than that, my Jude, I'm haunted by this dead man buried in San Pantalon. I'm doing it for this man who has no name, who had no proper mass said for him. I'm doing it for his children and his Penelope waiting and wondering, shamed by his absence and grieving for his return." Bigio picked up his walking stick, steeling himself for the mid-morning crowd in Campo San Polo.

Vegetable and fruit sellers, fishmongers, and butchers loudly manned their stalls. Hawkers of candied fruit and slices of polenta wove through the haggling crowd. Workmen grown infirm or injured and wives deserted and desperate scurried to the *magazzen* to pawn their rings and jewelry for cheap meat and borrower's wine. Traders whose ships were lost at sea or delayed in distant ports hurried into San Polo to pray for divine help. Barren women came to light candles and ask for a miracle, while the beneficiaries of life's good fortune gave thanks for God's grace. Ragged urchins stood at the church entrance and rubbed their stomachs with one dirty hand and held out the other for a few coins.

Bigio surveyed the stalls lining the large campo, looking for someone old enough to know all the people living around the campo, someone selling something that even an old courtesan fallen on hard times could afford to buy.

"Anna Ridolfi?"

The grizzled cheeked vegetable monger shook his head. "Not a name I know. What does she do?"

Now it was Bigio's turn to shake his head. "I don't know. She used to give pleasure."

"And never tires of telling you." He waved a clump of scallions toward the church entrance. "There she is, the one with tits like paddles, a martyr to Venus. The Duchess, that's the name she goes by here."

Bigio made out in the distance an indistinct figure sitting behind a basket of flowers. As he came closer he saw her cheeks spider-webbed and splotched crimson from years of malmsey and cheap Greek wine. She looked like a Carnival puppet with papier-mâché double chin and cheeks so swollen her dark eyes were small as coffee beans. When she smiled at passersby, there was a gap in the upper right side of her mouth where two teeth had been. Her face mapped the downward journey her life had taken. From a finely furnished apartment where she entertained patrician lovers to a shabby brothel in Castelletto where strangers known only by their first name came and went, then a narrow bed in a foul smelling room in the back of a *magazzen* where fuddled workmen and foreign sailors stuck their pricks quickly in and out, and finally, when wine and darkness could no longer hide the ravages of age and debauchery, she ended up here on campo stones, selling flowers, sleeping in the dark corners of churches, and jabbering about her perfumed past in water-shops and *malvasie* to anyone too drunk and tired to escape. Flower merchants sold her the blossoms their other customers wouldn't buy. She had her regulars, who stopped, offered a morning greeting, and bought a handful of her sad offerings. Bigio waited until no one stood by her basket.

"Anna?" Bigio's voice a comforting hush.

She looked up at him as if she were struggling to remember who that woman

was and who he might be. "You look familiar. Was I one of your favorites? Did we keep company?"

"I'm afraid not. Carla Franco favors me with her company."

"Oh, she's a beauty. The Duke had his eye on her. Said she was the second most beautiful woman in Venice." She laughed and shook her head back and forth, adrift for a moment in the past. "Still a beauty?"

"Yes, very much so."

"Some lovely flowers for Carla?" She held out a bunch of wilted gladiolas, black crescents of dirt under the nails of her thick fingers. Bigio said he was there to talk with her and could buy flowers or a glass of wine but not both. Wine being the milk of the old, her choice didn't surprise him. When mass was over and she sold out her basket, she would meet him at a *malvasie* a short walk from San Polo.

Bigio found a table far from the entrance. If any acquaintance walked by, they wouldn't see him in such a low place and think that poverty had driven him to malmsey and a common prostitute on a foul bed. She apologized for the surroundings. "When the Duke returns – and that will be any day now – you and I will converse in the cafés of San Marco where I was always treated with graciousness and respect."

The bones of the Duke, an Austrian with a noble name that meant nothing to Bigio, had likely been moldering in some crypt in Vienna for twenty years. For Anna he was alive, still fifty, handsome and ramrod regal in bearing. As soon as his affairs allowed, he would return for her. Poor creature, those who love foreigners love the wind.

Bigio told her that Father Zampelli of San Pantalon asked him to clear up some of Fumiani's affairs. "Carla says you knew him."

Her eyes lit up, her voice steadied, as she travelled back to honeyed memories. "That was a long time ago – I was beautiful then. I was a Virgin…" She saw the doubt on Bigio's face, smiled and took a sip of wine to draw the moment out. "…Mary. I'm in San Benedetto with the Saints."

"Carla said you were his model."

"And more … he was a married man in a cold bed. That was before the Duke. Once I met him, the Duke wanted all my time. I didn't tell the Duke. I had my secrets. It was my bed. Giovanni was a gentle man, not like the Duke, one minute sweet as sugar and the next angry as a wasp. Giovanni … he was a man more at home among angels and saints."

She sat quietly for a moment, lost in the past. "A sweet, sad man. He told me he shaved every night. Just in case. He didn't want his rough cheeks to scratch his wife's delicate skin. He didn't want her to turn away from his embrace."

She cost Bigio a second glass of cheap Greek wine and a cup of weak coffee that shamed the few beans used to make it. Her hand, red and scratched from jagged leaves and thorns, cradled the cheap wine like a prized vintage from the Veneto. The past was a land much more inviting than the hard stones of her current life. She roamed its mist-covered landscape with little coaxing. She didn't remember the year she first met gentle Giovanni. It must have been over twenty years ago, she said, she couldn't have been more than twenty-five years old. Drink and too many nameless men made her look like a crone of seventy, but Bigio figured she wasn't over fifty.

"He didn't talk much about his wife, and I didn't ask. Men came to escape, not to be reminded of the world outside the silk curtains of my bed."

It was difficult to imagine this hag a beautiful young woman who enticed with rouged cheeks and sweet words a faithful husband to her bed. She said at first Fumiani didn't sleep with her because she was too beautiful. "I can't sleep with the Virgin Mary, he said. I told him to think of me as his Mary Magdalene before the Savior touched her soul." She laughed, a slash of yellowed teeth and black gaps, "That made it easier."

She remembered his sad eyes that always seemed to be looking elsewhere. "Like he was in two places at the same time," she said. "Once he drew me while I lay sleeping. Just my head. Red chalk on light brown paper. He left it on the pillow. I found it when I awoke. What a gentle hand he had. You should have seen how beautiful I was. I've lost it…with all my moving about, all the deprivations Fortune has cast in my path." She sat silent for a moment, her lips trembling.

Anna couldn't remember when she last saw Fumiani. It was many years ago, when she had a grand home, a maid, silk pillows, and the company of the Duke. "He was one of the guilty ones. Said he should stop but kept coming back for my company. Finally, his visits became more irregular, then stopped altogether. Maybe it was money, maybe it was time. He didn't have much of either once he started painting the ceiling at San Pantalon. That's what he talked about all the time, the ceiling," she laughed with a foul-smelling cackle. "Sometimes when he lay spent next to me, his fingers drew patterns across my breasts and stomach. His fingers had a life of their own, drawing angels on my soft skin. I had soft skin then."

She pushed the empty glass toward the center of the table. "He's been dead for a while, hasn't he?"

"Four years."

"I wanted to go to the funeral mass but," her voice trailed off and she looked down at her dirty dress and chafed hands. "I go to San Pantalon ever so often, late in the day when they're few people around. It's like you're standing beneath the gates of heaven. My life hasn't been easy since the Duke left. Saint Pantalon looks after me." She paused and leaned forward across the table. "Do you believe in ghosts?"

"I've never seen one."

"I'm not sure," she said. "Last year on the Saint's feast day I was lighting a candle in one of the chapels, the one with the lovely painting of the saint healing the boy. I turned around and Giovanni was there, looking up at the ceiling. He was wearing a mask. He had a beard and his hair was down to his shoulders, but there was something about his hands. He was lifting a hand toward the ceiling like he was tracing figures in the air." She stared at the empty glass. "I never drink before I ask for Saint Pantalon's protection…I'm sure it was him. He looked my way then disappeared before I could call his name."

She reached down into the basket at her feet and picked up a few stray gladiolas crisscrossed at the bottom. "Give them to Carla. Tell her I'll pay her a visit when the Duke returns."

A noble savior, a devoted wife, a happy marriage, a strong and glorious Republic – how we cling to hollow myths, Bigio thought, to get us through our empty days. He dropped the withered flowers into the canal and limped back to his room, believing more firmly than ever that he would keep his promise to Carla. She wouldn't end her days begging for bread, church steps for a pillow.

13

Bigio made his way across the Rialto Bridge to the Angel apothecary to speak to Fumiani's father-in-law. The shop looked much like the Two Moors in San Barnaba where Bigio went for candles and soap and, when younger, medicine to relieve his frequent bouts of indigestion. Now he lived with his aches and pains. What time couldn't heal, he endured. Life taught him you might get better, but you would never get well.

Benches ran along both sides of the darkly paneled shop. At the far end a counter extended across its narrow width. A heavyset man in his middle years stood behind the counter. A modest-sized painting on wood of Mary and Joseph gently offering their blessing to the sick and anxious patrons of the Angel hung behind the counter in a rectangular alcove. On either side of the painting were shelves, floor to the rafters, lined with glass jars of paints and pigments, majolica vases of oil, syrup, sauces, and spices, flasks of distilled water and herbal remedies, and wooden boxes of pills and dried herbs. Bigio heard the pounding of pestles from a workroom hidden behind the shelves. Two young servants sat on the bench at the left waiting for their masters' orders to be filled. Three old men sat hip to hip across from them on the opposite bench, their gnarled hands cupped over walking sticks planted between their legs. The man in the middle was speaking, while the other two stared straight ahead. Tufts of white hair rang his bald head like a silver horseshoe. His face was heavily lined, his eyes, dark slits beneath wrinkled lids. He had the pale skin of a man who lived his life indoors. He didn't look up or stop talking as Bigio passed. Bigio asked the man behind the counter if he could speak to Angelo Taliaferro.

"Nicolas Taliaferro," he extended his hand. "That's my uncle." He tipped his head toward the elderly man who hadn't stopped talking since Bigio entered the apothecary.

"My uncle can't talk with you."

"I can wait until he's finished chatting with his friends."

"You don't understand."

Bigio turned to look again at the old man who stared into the distance as he spoke in a steady stream of sentences that at first hearing seemed the normal garrulousness of an idle old man. His words had the rhythm of sentences with pauses and full stops, the rise and fall of statements and questions, but as Bigio listened more closely the words made no sense. It was a crazy stew of words stumbling one after the other. One of his companions patted him gently on his knee, and the old man stopped speaking. After a few moments, he began again, a stream of senseless words.

"Does he know what he is saying?"

"I don't think so. His mind is a jumble. He can't understand what we're saying, that's for sure. You ask him a question or tell him to do something and he looks at you like you're an ignorant savage from the New World – he just carries on jabbering."

"What if I were to write something down?"

"That only agitates him. He knows he should be able to understand but he can't. This has been going on for almost two years, ever since his spell. I bring him here every day to keep my wife from throwing herself into the canal." Nicolas paused. "What's this all about?"

"Father Zampelli just wanted me to tie up some loose ends at San Pantalon."

Nicolas pointed to the painting behind the counter, "Giovanni painted that – a wedding gift to the family. He was a good man. Giovanni fell in love with Laura right here." He smacked his hand on the counter. "A blind man could see he was smitten. How couldn't he? An angel, ask anyone. God had a hand in that match. Giovanni adored her, and she believed he was destined for greatness."

Perhaps Nicolas felt he owed it to his uncle to be his voice, to praise his beautiful daughter and his famous son-in-law that brought fame to the family. Bigio looked at the old man, who for a moment was silent, his eyes darting about the shop, as if for a damning instant he understood the prison his addled mind had sentenced him to. Bigio let Nicolas talk.

Fumiani usually sent his apprentice to the Angel to buy his colors and linseed oil. The boy was a dreamer, his mind a colander. Orders and instructions flowed in and out like water. After bringing back the wrong color and totally forgetting the oil, Fumiani came himself. Back in those days his uncle kept a narwhal horn on a carved stand near the door as a curiosity to draw in customers. Two young girls no older than eight or nine, hands at their sides, stood near the open door staring at the narwhal horn towering above them. Laura came out from the workroom and saw the two girls. With her soft voice and gentle smile she enchanted them with tales of the unicorn's magical horn. She told the girls they could touch it. Shyly they reached out and rubbed their hands softly up and down the gleaming ivory. Nicolas said he didn't know who was more enchanted, the two girls or Fumiani. He lingered to sneak a glance at Laura, pretending to consider other colors to buy. With her unblemished cheeks, blue eyes, golden ringlets, and modest smile, she was, he told Nicolas later, more beautiful than any Virgin Mary by Bellini or Titian.

The next day Fumiani came back and instead of buying what he needed and leaving, he sat on the bench and chatted with the other customers – unusual, for Fumiani wasn't a man for idle chatter. He became quite forgetful over the next few weeks coming back for more pigment and walnut oil. His mother was suddenly afflicted by a torrent of minor ailments that required constant visits for a bit of *triaca*, a jar of honey, or a packet of pills. Laura's father offered his sympathies with a sly smile. Perhaps, he said, Fumiani best take his mother to the hospital for immediate attention.

Their courtship was short. Fumiani read the goodness of her soul in the beauty and grace of her face. Most of her friends were already married, and she didn't want to be an unmarried maid at twenty. She might have preferred someone younger than thirty-four, but her father assured her he was a man destined for renown. After the exchange of betrothal rings, Fumiani drew a rolled-up sheet of fine beige paper from a cloth bag he brought to the ceremony. He gave Laura a simple three-quarter portrait he had done of her, her face delicately rendered in red chalk and a touch of black chalk for her high collar and shoulders. She looked calm and self-assured. Her eyes pierced the distance.

"It was more beautiful than any painting I'd ever seen," Nicolas said with evident pride. "Laura was Giovanni's sun and moon. He painted her everywhere. It was easy to pick her out among the crowd kneeling before Mary and the infant Jesus, a beam of heavenly light setting her face aglow. She was a supplicant before Saint Roch, a luminous angel floating among the clouds, and the Virgin herself. Giovanni treated her well, gave her fine things, silk dresses, scarves, slippers sewn with pearls – whatever she wanted – though those things really didn't matter to her. His art was enough. Pity they didn't have any sons that could follow in his footsteps. That was a sadness for them both. When he fell, she died of a broken heart."

A happy marriage, a contented husband – these were rare birds seldom sighted in Venice. Happy men didn't run away from their lives. Bigio thanked Nicolas for his time and though the deaths were four years past, told him he was sorry for the family's loss.

"One last thing. Was there anyone who wished Fumiani ill?"

"Master Bigio, there are many people in Venice who like to make poison. Painters for all the beauty they create are a jealous lot, but I never heard anyone speak ill of Giovanni. It was an accident.

He worked too hard. It was the ceiling. The ceiling killed him. Have you talked to Busetto? He was an old friend of Giovanni's. Carlo Busetto, a fine painter of harpsichords and virginals. He has a workshop near San Angelo Raffaele. Talk to him, he knew him well. He will tell you the same."

Bigio said nothing. The ceiling may have killed someone, but not Fumiani.

A few people crossed the small campo in front of San Pantalon as Bigio walked toward the bridge over Rio Nuovo. He noticed a stocky man standing at the foot of the bridge. He was wearing a plain black mask and appeared to tip his head as if to acknowledge Bigio when he passed. The ragged lute player and his dog were in their usual spot on the other side of the bridge. Bigio heard the normally quiet dog growling and turned to see him baring his teeth as the masked man walked by. Midway down Campo San Margherita, Bigio sensed he was being followed. He stopped and turned around to see the masked fellow walking about ten yards behind. The man stopped but didn't look away or pretend to adjust his cloak or be interested in the goods offered in the nearby stalls. Bigio didn't feel threatened in the busy campo. He walked slowly towards home. Bigio pushed open the door to the palazzo and turned around again to see his masked shadow standing near the campo well staring at him. The man wanted to be seen. He wanted Bigio to know he was being followed.

14

Bigio rarely came to this part of the Dorsoduro where sign painters, furniture makers, and other craftsmen worked in small, cramped workshops along the Fondamenta Barbarigo. The double doors of Busetto's workshop were open to the fondamenta. Bigio smelled the turpentine, varnish, and paint a dozen steps away. Three men worked in a space crowded with frames and lids in various stages of preparation. A focused quietness enveloped the shop. Every man was absorbed in his work. Two young men, who looked to be in their early twenties, were at work in the back, one painting the plumage of a peacock on one lid, while the other outlined a trellis with flowers on another. For a moment Bigio was back in the family palazzo, sitting cross-legged on the floor, listening to his mother at a virginal painted ox-blood red that his father said came from a famous family of instrument makers in Antwerp. He remembered for the first time in many years the frolicking monkeys and rainbow-colored parrots that decorated the inside of the lid. He wondered what had come of it. His sister-in-law never showed much interest in music, only in the latest fashions from Paris and making his life unpleasant.

A thin man of medium height with a few sprigs of white hair above each ear stood at a table in the front of the workshop. Brush in hand, he bent over a misty mountain landscape on a virginal lid, humming silently to himself. Bigio stood at the threshold, not wanting to interrupt his concentration. After a few minutes, Carlo

Busetto looked up, put his brush down, and asked if there was something he could do for Bigio.

Bigio hid the purpose of his visit behind some vague parish affairs Father Zampelli had asked him to take care of. Busetto seemed a trusting soul who didn't question the motives of a priest and an old, lame patrician. Busetto had known "dear Giovanni" since they were ten-year-old boys in the studio of Francesco Alinari whose best days were then long past. Alinari claimed to have stood at the right hand of Vecellio, Titian's nephew, but likely, Busetto thought, he only cleaned brushes and daubed a distant mountain or a figure half hidden in shadow. Busetto, like an old soldier, seemed to revel in his youthful hardships. For five years he and Fumiani ground pigments and mixed colors till their forearms turned hard as oak and their shoulders ached. They boiled sizes, laid bole, and ground gesso. They spread a lagoon of glue and gesso and primed and stretched enough canvas to man the sails of a thousand Venetian galleys. They learned how to choose white hog bristles for the best brushes and how to cut a pen from a goose quill. He and Fumiani made brushes and cleaned crusty paint jars, carried wood, tended fires, and even ran errands to the market for Alinari's elderly wife. They copied drawings and drew hands, feet, arms, and well-muscled torsos from plaster models. They never painted from a live model or a cadaver. With Alinari it was just anatomical charts, jointed dolls, plaster models, cold marble, and rote learning. They sat quietly, pencil in hand, with a half dozen other apprentices while Alinari, perched on a high stool, recited over and over, in a voice like heavy boots on gravel, the laws of perspective and the orders of architecture and the rules of their use. They copied their master's works and learned later that Alinari sold them as his own hand and kept the money for himself.

"I knew early on that Giovanni was the star among us apprentices. I was sure he was destined for great things." Bigio let Busetto ramble on, letting him feel close once again to an old friend he admired and had looked up to. Fumiani's mother scrimped on lace and ribbons to buy her son chalk and good paper. She let him off from his chores in the kitchen for fear he might cut or burn his fingers. She was certain he was an instrument of God and would be another Tintoretto. More than once Busetto saw her press Fumiani's right hand between her two hands and kiss the tips of his blessed fingers.

When they walked through the crowded market stalls of the Rialto, Fumiani marked the faces of the women – their hair, their skin, their mouths – as they picked and poked fish flopping in crates at their feet and frowned at the price offered. He watched the movement of their hands as they dug into their purses for stubborn coins, the flash of their eyes as they bargained, and how they held their bodies as they wove in between the people clumped in front of the stalls. He paid special attention to the shifting shadows cast by the stall awnings on their shawls and blouses, how the colors of their garments changed as they moved between light and shadow. How the slivery blue and gray scales of the fish glistened in the sunlight. He saw the outline of Fumiani's fingers in the pocket of his jacket as he rolled a pencil between thumb and index finger, anxious to return home, and draw what he had seen in the journal he kept on the floor by his bed. Fumiani, Busetto laughed, ate bread in one hand, and drew with the other.

He remembered the day Fumiani told him he wanted to do more than paint works for chapel wall or altar. Fumiani and his father were walking in the morning near the church of San Giovanni Elemosinario, a small church squeezed into a wall of buildings so hidden behind a row of market stands that only its parishioners could find it. They met an old glazier who was a friend of Fumiani's father. Though over seventy, the glazier was a man much in demand for his skill in cutting and fitting windows of any shape or size. When his father told the glazier that his son was apprenticing with Alinari, the man put his hand on Fumiani's shoulder and told him he wanted to take him to heaven. A few days before, a freakish hailstorm cracked three of the four rectangular windows under the dome of San Giovanni Elemosinario. A scaffold was put under the cupola in the center of the nave. The glazier took the boy's hand and led him carefully up a zigzag of ladders into the pink-tinged clouds of heaven. A circle of cherubs floated among the clouds in dizzying abandon above Fumiani's head. He wanted to jump up and grab a cherub's hand and frolic with him among the receding rings of clouds. Fumiani couldn't stop smiling with joy. Anything for chapel or palazzo walls no matter the subject, size, or gilded frame paled against the heavenly expanse a ceiling offered. He wouldn't be content until he flew among the angels. Anyone could paint a ceiling, Fumiani wanted to paint heaven. He wanted the faithful to stand open-mouthed and clear-eyed beneath heaven's infinite majesty.

Fumiani became upset when people spoke of quadratura as a bag of tricks, as if he were a Carnival magician pulling coins from behind the ears of small children. He was proud of all that he learned in his five years in Bologna: architectural orders, the laws of mathematics, the rules of symmetry and perspective, the buildings of the ancient Greeks and Romans, and the arts of poetic invention. Not any painter, no matter his skill at figures, could extend the architectural elements of real space into the imagined space of the ceiling and weave heaven and earth together in one grand illusion of infinite space. Busetto wanted Bigio to know how difficult it was to paint such a vast painting on canvas. What might seem like broad, crude strokes a few feet away had to have a lively, natural appearance when seen from the church floor. Fumiani compared different types of canvas and chose the same heavy canvas of coarse hemp that Tintoretto used when painting large works viewed from a distance. Fumiani constructed small models in wax and clay, dressed them with pieces of cloth, and arranged them in perspective boxes made of pasteboard cut with little windows so he could observe the effect of light and shadow. He hung miniature wax figures from the beams in his studio and lay on the floor watching them as they moved in the draughts whistling through the loose windows.

Busetto visited Fumiani in his studio when he painted the canvases for San Pantalon and went to the church to watch his friend at work high up on the scaffolds. The ceiling wasn't just another commission to keep his larder full. It was more than decoration to please the eye. Fumiani wanted the faithful to shudder at Pantalon's suffering, to wait in anguished anticipation while the emperor considered Pantalon's fate, and feel their souls soar as angels swooped down to welcome the blessed martyr.

The rebuilding of the church went slowly and the raising of the funds even slower. The priest was going bald with anxiety and hard work, wringing ducats from many good hearts. Francisco Comino, the architect, was afraid he would never see his plans completed. Fumiani worried his own health would give out before he finished the ceiling. He had no sons to carry on his work if he faltered. His fingers would become crooked and arthritic as Saint Francis, his body shriveled as Saint Jerome in the desert. He would totter up the scaffold, afraid to look down for fear of losing his balance and tumbling to his death.

"Yes," Busetto said, "late at night, beset by worries and unable to sleep, Giovanni had premonitions of falling." He hesitated, his voice an almost mournful hush, "Giovanni told me only death would keep him from finishing the ceiling."

"A very ambitious man," Bigio said.

"Yes, but for God not himself, at least in the beginning."

"In the beginning?"

Busetto paused, "Before he married Laura. She was a beautiful woman. I don't like to speak ill of the dead." He paused again, Bigio thought out of kindness more for his friend than his wife. "Giovanni wanted to paint well. Laura wanted to live well. Giovanni wanted a soft bed and a full larder, but the rest was little matter to him. Laura thought him destined for greatness.

She wanted to live like the most praised painters of Venice with liveried servants, fine tapestries, and gilded mirrors on the walls." Busetto hesitated, reluctant to besmirch the memory of his friend. "Sometimes I think my friendship embarrassed her. I didn't always feel welcome in her home."

Bigio, an exile from the home of his birth, felt a kinship to this gentle soul. "Why?"

"I wasn't a painter."

Bigio looked at the harpsichord lids with their luminous blue skies and nymphs and gods sporting amidst green hills dotted with poplar and pine. "I don't understand."

"Master Bigio, I was not in the College of Painters."

Bigio looked blankly at Busetto, the answer making no sense to him. "You put brush to paint and paint to canvas, plaster, or wood. That makes you a painter."

Busetto shook his head, "Not in Venice," he said. "In Bologna painters had their own academy. Here painters revered for their works in church and palazzo were lumped together with practitioners of the mechanical crafts – painters of musical instruments like myself, gilders, textile designers, embroiderers, leather workers." He paused, counting the others on his fingers, "Makers of playing cards and masks, stationers, miniaturists, sign painters, house painters, and painters of leather and wax fruit. When Fumiani returned he was among the many painters who petitioned the Senate for a separate academy. They settled for a guild, but at least they were no longer thrown in with their lowly artisan cousins.

"I'm an artist. Giovanni knew that. In her heart I think Laura did too. She just wanted her husband to be recognized and rewarded." He motioned toward a harpsichord lid drying against the wall, "I'm no sign painter. Look, tell me that's not beautiful. I put my soul into it. That's what makes it art. I have brought beauty into the world. And…" he laughed, "I married off my two daughters to decent fellows."

Bigio saw nothing gained for the moment in troubling this

good man with the truth about his friend, or the only truth that he knew. It would only cause him pain to learn his friend abandoned him and for three years lived a short gondola ride away across the Giudecca Canal.

"I'm sorry I didn't see much of Giovanni the last year before his death. The ceiling was his life." Busetto rubbed his eyes with the back of his hand. "I never told Giovanni that he was right – he did paint heaven."

Yes, Bigio thought, he did paint heaven. But however grand it was, it was an illusion. There were no angels in the reality below, just flawed humans stumbling their way through the murk and muck that no amount of glaze and colors could brighten.

15

Bigio didn't think a poor old patrician chatting with a fruit-seller would draw the attention of the Republic's spies. The old lingered in the markets. They had no place to go, no business to transact, no one who needed to hear what was on their minds. They complained about the damp weather over a crate of silvery butterfish flopping their last breath. They stood by a pyramid of polished plums and remembered when young men dressed like men and young brides had reputations unblemished as the pearls that hung around their necks. Who else would listen to them besides their songbirds and hazy apparitions from their past that only they could see?

"Try this plum." Pietro handed Bigio a firm purple plum. Pietro leaned over with a conspiratorial tilt of his head and spoke in a hushed voice. "I get only the best."

Everyone in the market knew that Pietro's sister-in-law's cousin in Mira sold him plums, cherries, and figs directly from his orchard. He made arrangements every year before the harvest and didn't have to go through the official channels the government required. He played at the edge of the law, but he wasn't the only one. Those that grumbled, he told Bigio many times, would do the same if they had the connections.

"I want to make my customers happy." He patted Bigio on the shoulder.

"You need to be careful, Pietro."

"You too. People are asking questions. What is that Bigio up to? Why is he disturbing the dead?"

Bigio didn't want to disturb the dead. He wanted the dead to rest in peace, their bones buried where they belonged. He wanted the dead to have a name and someone to pray for his soul. "What kind of people?"

Pietro pointed in the direction of San Marco and the Ducal Palace. "People who don't like to be disturbed." He turned solemn. His fruit monger's smile disappeared. He motioned toward the Scuola dei Varotari at the end of the campo where rotting fruit and vegetables and other market refuse were piled against one wall, "People who know how to get rid of the garbage."

An old woman pushed past Bigio and began to haggle with Pietro over a handful of figs. He brought down the price a bit at no great loss, and she left nodding her head in victory.

"Master Bigio, after I finish packing things away, meet me in San Benedetto. You and I should pray to the Virgin Mary for protection."

Bigio paused by the well in front of San Benedetto to catch his breath. Pietro could have sought the Virgin's help closer to San Margherita. Bigio guessed he had more on his mind than divine protection. Bigio had walked by the church many times on his way to the nearby palazzos on the Grand Canal, but he didn't remember ever going in. It was as if he was seeing the church for the first time. Strange, he thought, how you live your life so inattentive to the world around you, how you pass by places that line the stations of your life without notice.

The afternoon sky turned overcast. Dim light bathed the nave. Wisps of candle smoke floated in the side chapels. Pietro was in a side chapel midway down the nave on the left leaning against a thick column looking at a painting of the Virgin above the chapel altar.

"She looks like my sister," he said.

Pietro swore at times like a Turk. His crude wit sometimes made

Bigio blush. Bigio waited for a joke about Pietro's sister's virginity or its loss, but Pietro only stared at the painting. A serene Virgin stood above an arc of four figures, saints most likely, who looked up at her in calm expectation, waiting perhaps for her blessing. Something might happen, but it would happen later.

"Fumiani, he was a master. Even a poor fellow like me can see that."

It was the first time Pietro had mentioned the painter's name. He smiled, "I have fruit to sell, but I have friends with big ears and time to lounge about the Broglio. People ask questions, it's Venice. Suspicions and rumors, they're our daily bread. People wanted to know why the hurry. Why was such a great artist buried so quickly and with no ceremony at all?" Pietro leaned closer, his voice low. "If he fell, someone pushed him. Or loosened a board."

Pietro and men of his rank supped on conspiracy. Accidents didn't happen to great men. A carpenter might fall from scaffolding, a drunken cobbler end up floating in the canal one night. A patrician or citizen of some repute didn't suffer the accidents and indignities that lesser men did. Greatness made them the victims of conspiracy and intrigue. Caesar couldn't have been slain by Brutus alone.

It wasn't that Bigio didn't trust Pietro. He had helped him before. He could, when the situation demanded it, be secretive as a mole. Life taught Bigio if you wanted a man as your ally, it was better not to tell him the truth, partial as it might be, but let him find it out for himself. Let him feel he owned the truth. If you wanted him to keep his eyes open, better that he thought he was opening yours. "Who would want to kill Fumiani?"

"I don't know, but I know some people who might over a glass or two of wine. The workers at San Pantalon and other common folk are more comfortable speaking to the likes of me. Nothing personal."

"Pietro, why do you want to help me?"

He nodded toward Bigio's legs. "Master Bigio, no insult

intended, but a man of your age and condition needs a friend if he wants to find out the truth of this affair. This is an old house, and you know an old house never lacks a rat."

"Pietro, if a rat is gnawing at the timbers, I wouldn't want you to be crushed in the collapse. Where would I get my fruit?" Bigio said with a smile. "Why does Fumiani matter to you?"

"Master Bigio, I might give you and some other folks a free plum or peach once in a while, but people have to pay for what they get, or the world would stop spinning. Some people in the Republic think they can go through life without paying. I might stretch things a bit, but I'm an honest man. If someone killed a great man like Fumiani, they should pay."

"Pietro, I didn't know you were a man of such high principles."

"Oh, you mean justice or honor. I leave that to noblemen like you. I don't have the luxury to worry about those things – I have a wife and daughter to feed and another in the oven. I'm not a man who bites his nails with envy. That's not to say I don't take pleasure in giving a poke in the eye to those busybodies in the Palace with all their rules who make it hard for an honest man to make a decent living."

"Be careful."

"Master Bigio, don't you worry. Old Pietro can take of himself. I know good fruit from bad."

16

"What news, Stefano?"

"Nothing yet. Being dead for four years is a long time." It wasn't that Bigio didn't trust Zampelli. He owed Fumiani his silence. He wanted the full truth before maligning the man's memory. Ambition, a desire for greatness and perfection, loving a vain woman: they were no sins, just the shared failings of men.

"You know Venice. Spies and loose tongues. Word will get out. Better to have answers before we drown in a flood of rumors, half-truths, and wild speculation. Have you talked with Zaccaria Sagredo? He was an enthusiastic patron of Fumiani. Oh, and Stefano, a prayer to Saint Pantalon. That will help. Giovanni prayed every day to Saint Pantalon for good health so he could finish the ceiling."

A lot of good that did, Bigio thought.

"His wife worried about his health. I guess every woman married to an older man does. She rarely came to see how the ceiling was coming along. Said the dust bothered her eyes. I think his working up on the scaffold frightened her. She couldn't bear to look. He could have had assistants up there doing the work, but it was his ceiling he said. He told me when his work was done he would go to Ravello to see the saint's blood come alive on his feast day and give thanks for allowing him to finish the ceiling." Zampelli's voice quavered. He gulped, shaken by thanks never given.

Zampelli recovered his composure and eagerly told Bigio about his own visit to Ravello soon after coming to San Pantalon. He traveled there with a party of Venetian priests and noblemen, including a cousin of the dogaressa Elisabetta Querini – a fine young fellow, Zampelli said. Blessed was the pious lady of Nicomedia who gathered Pantalon's blood and milk mixed with the soil on which it fell, squeezed it into a flask, and kept it safe in her home. Now pilgrims came every year to the Cathedral of St. Pantalon to witness the miracle of the blood.

A carnival of hawkers peddling colored water and false elixirs to cripples and the infirm crowded the cathedral steps. To Zampelli's relief, a hushed solemnity reigned once inside the church. They walked up a narrow stairway one at a time to a platform on the outer wall of the Chapel of the Blessed Sacrament. Through a square opening cut in the wall he saw a narrow necked glass flask held between two iron clasps, protected front and back by a gilt iron railing. The light was dim. The platform didn't allow for more than a dozen pilgrims at a time. The blood of the saint bubbled red as rubies in the sealed flask. The walls of the church disappeared. Zampelli felt he was standing in ancient Nicomedia at the saint's martyrdom, the blood and milk from Pantalon's severed neck pouring on the ground in front of his own feet. He felt Christ hovering above him. He and the pilgrims crowded around him trembled in awe, overwhelmed by the miracle they were witnessing. They embraced, friend and stranger, tears streaming down their cheeks.

Skeptics and heretics claimed it was the light, the air, even the heat from the pilgrim's bodies, or worse the chicanery of the priests that caused the thick mix of dirt, dried blood, and milk that normally filled half the flask to bubble to the brim. Zampelli's eyes glistened at the memory of the miracle seen with his own eyes: the flask, untouched by human hands, full and bubbling crimson clear as red wine.

If Bigio prayed, he would pray for the priest's unquestioning faith. Bigio wanted to believe in miracles. Miracles gave people hope. But blood bubbling every year on the same day sounded like a Carnival mountebank's trickery. The blood of the saint gathered up from ground where he was beheaded and saved for over a thousand years was a tale too neat to be true. Priest, painters, and poets celebrated the miracles of God. They left unmarked the miracles of ordinary folk with their faults and foibles who struggled to be decent in a corrupt world.

17

Sagredo's houseboy brought a note written in a fine hand inform-
ing Bigio that his master would see him in four days when all
the planetary aspects were in alignment but not before noon and
not until after his midday meal. Bigio had never meet Zaccaria
Sagredo, latest and likely the last Sagredo. The Sagredo name was
one of the first to be written in the Golden Book. They hadn't
recently discarded their dirty aprons to buy their way into the pages
of the patricians.

The Sagredo palazzo shone in white marble purity on the Grand
Canal. Its opulent interior brought back memories of the luxurious
life Bigio had lost. As a boy he stood on the balcony looking out on
the Grand Canal and watched the ships heading to sea and profits,
believing his future was bright as their sunlit sails. Brandishing
a child's wooden sword he slid across the polished *portego* floor
slaying the enemies of the Republic lurking behind the full regalia
of the family armor sparkling in the morning light. The crystal
flowers and scalloped leaves of chandeliers glowed above marble
mantelpieces. Taffeta curtains floated like green waves against the
windows. Charity flanked by Patience, Justice, Hope, and Faith
benevolently gazed down from coffered ceilings. In the optimism
of youth he never thought that he would end his years alone with
Charity and Patience, long ago deserted by Hope and Faith.

Sagredo sat on a brocaded divan in a drawing room off the
portego. A bachelor in his late fifties, he was a small man with delicate features whose pale skin had the pallor of someone who rarely

ventured out before sunset. He wore a powdered white periwig and his smooth cheeks were slightly rouged. He reminded Bigio of the small glass figures the craftsmen of Murano made for the pleasure of young girls. Though the afternoon heat was heavy in the room, he was dressed in a patrician gown lined in ermine. Youthful gods frolicked in fleshy abandon by sylvan brooks on richly colored Belgian tapestries, angels and putti floated among clouds thick as whipped cream on the gilded ceiling, and naked Greek youths admired their marble beauty in gilded mirrors. Sagredo rose slowly and walked a few careful steps towards Bigio as if his slippered feet were truly made of glass. Bigio caught the faint scent of rosewater.

"May I offer you something to refresh yourself?" he pointed to a pitcher on a round marble top table. "I always add a drop of aniseed to the *acquaioli*. It makes it so much more refreshing." He spoke in a formal way as if he were reciting the words of a play he had memorized. His slender fingers trembled as he poured the cloudy liquid into a delicate flute with translucent green leaves at its stem.

"You wish to speak of poor dear Fumiani?"

"Father Zampelli tells me you knew him well."

"Oh no," his fingers tugged at his collar, "it is his art that I know well. Long after you and I, Stefano, have sailed away, people will travel here to look up in awe at the magnificent apotheosis of Saint Pantalon. It is a wonder of the world, a glorious expression of man's artistic soul. Don't you agree?"

"I rarely look up, it hurts my neck."

"Oh my, Stefano, don't say that. You sound like those foreign Philistines who go to San Sebastiano and the Scuola San Rocco and complain they grow dizzy looking up too long with their heads tilted back. How can one make his way on this earth without looking up at the stars?" He tugged again at the collar of his gown. "I could not live without art. What an empty existence. I would rather waste away than go one day without beauty. Art ... is," he put a finger to his pursed lips, searching for the *bon mot*, "God speaking through the hand of man."

The paintings and tapestries that surrounded Bigio in his youth were simply the taken-for-granted decorations befitting a patrician family of long standing. They were family possessions handed down from generation to generation that he knew at an early age would be his brother's and not his. His father scolded Bigio when he touched the tapestries with fingers sticky with toffee and warned him not to play too close to the paintings' gilded frames. His father never spoke of the pleasure the art gave him.

When Pietro held a ripe plum between his fingers and turned it slowly to show its smooth purple skin, Bigio understood the pleasure the fruit monger took in its firm fleshed perfection. Words about art rang hollow to him. They were weightless and unmoored, floating in a world unconnected to the objects and emotions they were intended to describe. Yes, Bigio admired the Virgin rising heavenward in I Frari, but no currents of emotion bore him aloft with her. He stood looking up at her, red paint on canvas, his faith placid as ever. He turned and walked down the nave and out into the campo and headed for San Marco for a good cup of coffee, the stink of the canal in his nostrils.

"You must see Fumiani's other work – San Zaccaria, San Benedetto …" Sagredo paused to remember more, "San Rocco of course, San Moisè. More water?" Bigio waved his hand no.

"Some who should know better think with Titian's passing that the light of Venice was extinguished. That the age of giants has passed. How can one look up at Saint Pantalon and speak of decay and decline? Fumiani was a giant, a master of illusion." Sagredo paused, taking a deep breath to steady himself. "You can see that I am not in robust health. The moist air makes my blood run languid. Mosquitoes have given up tormenting me in search of prey with thicker blood. I don't venture out often among the jostling crowds in San Marco. I cannot bear the unsavory foreigners who cough and spit without regard for those standing nearby. All those unruly fellows pushing and shoving to watch dancing bears and other coarse pleasures. The screech of the knife grinder's wheel on the Rive Schiavone disturbs my humors. But I cannot let a week go by without going to San Pantalon to marvel at Fumiani's vision, to have my faith girded by the saint's glorious martyrdom."

"It was an unfortunate accident," Bigio said.

"Very unfortunate, but an accident? I am not so sure."

Zampelli had said nothing about Sagredo's suspicions. Bigio read too many faces not to know Sagredo had something on his mind. "What do you mean?"

Sagredo lowered his voice as if spies were hiding behind the silk curtains. "Murder."

"You think someone pushed him off the scaffold."

"Pushed maybe, loosened boards perhaps." He grew animated, color working its way from his neck to his forehead until his pale skin turned a throbbing pink. "Didn't Zampelli tell you? He might call them accidents. A broken armature, scaffolding that tumbled to the floor, a canvas panel found frayed and ripped, a small fire among oily rags. One event, you call it an accident, one after the other every four or five months, it becomes an incident, a pattern that cannot be dismissed. There was a carpenter working on the scaffolding who was slashed badly one evening in the Campo Margherita. They never found his assailants. And the graffiti, didn't Zampelli tell you of the desecration?"

Bigio shook his head and waited for Sagredo to continue weaving a conspiracy that explained the great artist's death. A giant didn't just stumble from a scaffold that had been his second home for years. Pietro wasn't alone mired in the swamp of conspiracy. It was a Venetian malady. Great men were felled by the acts of evil men not weak timbers or the inattention of God.

"One morning in Carnival a few months before Giovanni perished, someone painted on the church doors and the door of Fumiani's studio *"Papalisti"* in large crude red letters. San Pantalon was the only church desecrated. Some dismissed it as the drunken work of youthful revelers, but why not something more anatomical, more vulgar as is the usual vandalism of the young?"

"Excuse me, I don't understand what this has to do with Fumiani."

"He painted like a Roman."

"'Painted like a Roman,' what does that mean? And whatever it means, why would anyone want to kill him for that?"

"Paolo Sarpi was set upon by Roman assassins three times."

Every citizen of Venice knew of Sarpi's patriotic defense of the Republic against the Pope's interference, but that was over a century ago. Much more was at stake than a painting in a small parish church: papal interdiction, matters of state, and control over the Republic's religious affairs. Sagredo leaned back, his thin, finely tapered fingers tugging again at his collar. He spoke in a low, avuncular voice as if Bigio were a young man unschooled in the ways of the world. "In affairs of faith, memories are long, ill will bequeathed from generation to generation. Suspicion of papal intentions runs thick in Venetian blood. The Jesuits were allowed back over fifty years ago, and the Dominicans still hiss and snarl at them from the pulpit."

Bigio struggled to hide his impatience at being led astray into a swamp of conspiratorial mud and weeds. "Fumiani was a Venetian born and never went to Rome as far as I've heard."

"True, Stefano. He never spoke in favor of Rome in my presence. We only spoke of simple matters of faith, of how he could best strengthen the faith of the flock with his art. He was a man of deep faith. It was not a cloak he wore lightly draped over his shoulders. Pardon me, Stefano, but you do not seem a man much moved by the glorious art that surrounds us. Why, I will leave for another afternoon's chat. But there are many among us for whom art is a matter of life…and death."

Bigio couldn't imagine this nervous, frail fellow slitting a man's throat or pouring a vial of poison into a goblet for the sake of a painting. Though perhaps, blinded by covetousness, Sagredo might pay someone to push a rival collector off a bridge on a dark night.

"Oh, I don't mean we patrons of the arts are murderous creatures. Heavens no. That's not what I mean. What I do mean is there are men in the Senate who consider the Papacy a power hostile to the interests of our Republic with such bitter vehemence that that they despise all things Roman. Their anti-Roman sentiments extend even to the ceiling of our humble San Pantalon. They saw Fumiani's masterful illusionism as a detestable expression of Roman art. They lumped poor Fumiani with the Jesuit extravagance and excess of Fra Pozzo whose work in Rome is much praised by those with unbiased eyes. Maybe someone wanted to frighten him, warn him off from doing anything like it again. Maybe they pushed too hard and he stumbled. I don't know, Stefano. What I do know, what is beyond dispute, is that a healthy man at the pinnacle of his powers, comfortable on a scaffold, falls to his death just as he is about to finish his masterpiece. God does not have such a cruel sense of humor."

What Bigio knew beyond dispute was that it wasn't Fumiani who fell to his death. It would get him no closer to learning the name of the dead man to tell Sagredo that truth. Let him believe what he wanted to believe. It gave order to his world. He was a man in need of order to calm his nervous disposition. At least if what he said was true, Fumiani was not a murderer, and Zampelli would be relieved. Maybe the assassins killed a workman to send a message to Fumiani, or they were tormentors sent to frighten Fumiani, as Sagredo believed, and mistook a workman for the painter. In either case, a frightened Fumiani fled out of fear for his life. This explanation might fit the circumstances. That didn't mean it was true. It seemed to Bigio an ill-fitting garment.

"Who in this anti-Rome faction would go so far?"

"I cast my votes on Sunday and return home. I don't linger outside the palace exchanging gossip, Stefano. Our cruder citizens use its pillars as a place to relieve themselves. The stench is quite unpleasant. Ask Father Zampelli, he follows the machinations of the Broglio with great interest. Be careful though, you may not want to poke a hornet's nest."

"Who else might have wanted to harm Fumiani? Perhaps someone who thought he sold him a fake or cheated him with inferior work. I've heard painters in the Republic weren't above such practices."

Sagredo's face and neck reddened. "Not Fumiani. He was a most diligent and honest man. Stefano, have you read Vasari?" Bigio shook his head no. "I commend it, most worthwhile. Fumiani was very much a student of his work. He read that Michelangelo made a cap of thick paper and put a candle atop it so he could work late into the night. Fumiani did the same for God and his dear wife. It is true there are men in the Republic who succumb to greed and who shame the name artist. They charge by the figure and stuff their paintings full of them. They devise elaborate calculations to wring coins from a patron's purse. Three putti equal one figure or five seraphs heads are worth a figure and even charge by the number of buildings, hills, valleys, and the horses pulling a chariot. Not Fumiani. He was never one of those who say, 'I paint what I'm paid,' and leave the Christ child orphaned in an empty sky without a gloria of angels because he thought the patron's price too meager. He never dashed off lifeless portraits of saints like loaves of bread for the tourist trade. Not dear Fumiani. He was not one of those who fake old masters with deceitful games – painting over old panels, darkening new canvas with smoke. Though many do, as far as I know Fumiani never wasted his time making copies of his own works. Those who paint for today are forgotten tomorrow." Sagredo's shoulders sagged and his delicate hands trembled. "All this greed exhausts me."

Sagredo rose to signal that their conversation was over. He walked to the door, and then stopped. "Before you go, there is something I want you to see."

Bigio followed Sagredo down the *portego* slashed with late

afternoon sun into a bedroom more opulently decorated than the drawing room. The walls were covered in light green floral brocade. More than twenty stucco cherubs floated from the wall and ceiling of the antechamber and the bed alcove. There was a large bed wide enough for Sagredo and two frolicking companions with a cut velvet crimson headboard edged in gilt. Above the bed all done in stucco was a circular recess garlanded with flowers where cherubs playfully floated entwined in thick tasseled ribbons. Artful objects of gold, silver, crystal, and precious stones covered two marble topped console tables and a dresser. The room smelled of sandalwood and mingled fragrances of an almost overpowering sweetness. Sagredo picked up a small silver cup from the top of one of the tables, "Nero sipped wine from this." He put it down and with both hands gently picked up a small red vase with a thin, delicate neck. He held it up to the light. "The Emperor of China admired this vase and held it in his hands just like this." He placed the vase gently back atop the table and walked to the antechamber window and pulled back the curtain. Motes of dust danced in the sunlight. "I know what you must be thinking. I am ill with collecting, like a drunkard his wine, a concupiscent old man his young courtesans, a gambler at the tables at the Ridotto. No, this is much different. They wake up in the morning with a headache, the pox, or an empty purse, while I have these works of beauty to fill my life with joy."

And then, Bigio said to himself, you die, just like the drunkard, the whoremonger, and the gambler. A witless notary, his breath rank with garlic and cheap wine, will pick up the porcelain vase with ink-stained fingers and clumsily set it down hard on the table, entering in his ledger that it's a dull piece bought from a stall at the Festa della Sensa for a few ducats.

Sagredo swung his hand toward a large painting in a gild frame on the wall opposite the bed, "Fumiani. Come look at it in sunlight. You cannot judge women or paintings by the light of a candle." Sagredo tittered at his witticism. It was unlikely, Bigio thought, that any woman had ever come to this bed. Perhaps beardless boys. On second thought, not even young boys – they might break something.

The painting seemed to Bigio a plain and placid work. The colors were pale pinks and browns, dull whites and reds. Not much was happening, little to hold the eye. A bearded man, his hand on a table, bent over, to listen to the words of a large angel with golden ringlets, while two other angels eavesdropped on the conversation.

"I commissioned it, *Abraham and the Three Angels*. You know the story of course."

"They've come to tell him they will destroy Sodom and Gomorrah."

"Stefano, you view the world so darkly, you see only the shadows."

"Clearly, not darkly. I see the world as it is."

"I see the good news the angel brings – the son Sarah will bear despite her advanced years. This is not a scene that portends death and destruction. It heralds life and redemption. God's redemptive grace. It is the last thing I see before I fall asleep and the first thing I see when I awake."

Sagredo stepped back and gazed at the painting. "The faces of these angels bring me such peace. Stefano, have you heard of a Roman painter called Caravaggio?

"My ignorance extends well beyond the boundaries of Venice."

"This Caravaggio found his models in the alleys of Rome and made beggars saints, and whores virgins. Fumiani's angels come from heaven itself."

Sagredo stood silently in front of his angels for a few more moments. "I gave them their own wall. I wanted the painting to breath, to give it room to speak. These new nobles fresh to the Golden Book," he shook his head side to side with evident disdain, "fill their walls with pictures from floor to ceiling. Pictures that should be hung high are hung low, and those that should be seen straight on need a spyglass to be seen at all. They cover the walls with more bad pictures than good, hoping to hide their shallow lineage under yards of canvas." Agitated he pulled an embroidered handkerchief from his sleeve and wiped his forehead.

Bigio looked at the painting a bit longer to give Sagredo the impression that he shared his enthusiasm. He asked out of politeness if had others.

"A few drawings that's all. I wish I had more, but I could not compete with the Grand Prince of Tuscany. When he was not painting the ceiling, Fumiani was painting for the Prince."

Years after his last Carnival visit Venetians still talked of Ferdinando de Medici's time in the city. There was no pleasure he hadn't enjoyed, no desire left unsatiated. All of Venice knew of the young boys whose company he enjoyed, his scandalous affair with Cecchino, and how he returned to Florence with the sweet-voiced castrato in tow. His love of opera led him into the beds of La Bambagia and La Bombace, whose husband was not pleased but had no choice but to play the cuckold in silence.

The Prince didn't pay a visit to Carla. He sought more youthful company of both sexes, she told Bigio. But she heard that he was a man of refined musical taste and ability, with a lovely voice in the higher registers when in the throes of pleasure. He returned to Florence with floppy stockings and the gift of the pox.

"I didn't know that the Grand Prince was a regular visitor to the city."

"He isn't, but Cassana buys on his behalf." Sagredo pursed his lips as if he were sucking a slice of lemon. Cassana was another name that meant nothing to Bigio. "I calumniate no man, but he's a coarse and hot-tempered Genoan of mediocre ability. A pushy fellow. Rumor is he sent his self-portrait unbidden to the Prince. How he talked his way into the good graces of the Prince I do not know, but now he thinks himself a Medici. A fly on the axle of the royal chariot that takes credit for the dust whipped up by the spinning wheels. He lives off the Prince and copies of old masters he fobs off to naïve Englishmen as originals at exorbitant sums. A shoddy piece of work this fellow."

"Where can I find this Cassana?"

"Strutting about in San Zulian somewhere."

Bigio thanked Sagredo for his hospitality and parted with pleasantries and a promise to continue their talk of art and beauty on his next visit.

Outside the sky was darkening. The stench of the canal had grown stronger.

Discarded scraps of basketry and pieces of broken wood floated alongside a battered skiff in the narrow canal running by the Sagredo palazzo. They fooled the eye, and at first glance Bigio thought the boat itself was floating toward the Grand Canal, but looking again, he saw it was moored, going nowhere. Bigio too was stranded, caught in an eddy of rumor and conspiracy, nothing more than the flotsam and jetsam of a decaying city. He might be a Philistine when it came to painted walls and ceilings, but it made no sense that a cultured man like Sagredo believed someone would be killed over painted columns and angels swirling among clouds in a make-believe heaven. The truth floated by, unseen and out of reach under the dark, dirty water.

18

Three ragged urchins stood on the steps blocking Bigio's way. They gave him sullen looks and barely moved when he tried to shoo them away. Young boys usually played their games in the center of the campo. Today it was filled with a raucous throng. The boys didn't want to lose the vantage point they had claimed to watch the festivities. It wasn't every day that a resident of the campo was led to San Marco to be hung. The candied fruit sellers were doing good business.

The crowd hooted for blood and damned to hell the poor seamstress who poisoned her husband, a caulker at the Arsenal. Rumor was she grew tired of his slaps and punches, while some said she had a young lover in Campo Carmini and wanted to rid herself of her loutish husband. Whatever her motives, she killed her husband, and now she stood near the steps of the church facing the campo well. Soon she would be food for crows. Beheaded, her body would be hacked to pieces and left to rot throughout the city. A somber priest and hooded members of the Scuola San Fantin in their ceremonial black cowls lined up in front and behind the murderess ready to accompany her to the Columns of Justice in San Marco. Bigio saw above the heads of the crowd the large silver cross, gilded angels, ceremonial sword glinting in the sunlight, and the processional standards carried by the members of the Scuola. Atop the last standard a carved and painted Man of Sorrows looked down on his fallen flock unredeemed by his sacrifice. When Bigio was a boy, a bit older than the ones crowded on his steps, he stood, as most young boys did at least once, in San Marco as the Maleficio pealed for the condemned, and justice was done. One beheading was enough for him. The murderess stood dazed with pain, the front of her rough cotton smock stained red by her bloody hand that hung around her neck. Bigio turned away.

Pietro's daughter had come the day before with a message from her father, "Important news." Bigio gave her a red glass gem for a task well done. She clutched it tight in her hand. He called after her to be careful as she skipped down the stairs. If he had known the procession would take place that afternoon, he would have sent word to Pietro that he couldn't meet him again at San Benedetto. Bigio stepped cautiously out into the jostling crowd. One of the boys, upset at being displaced from his perch and excited by the blood lust of the crowd, followed behind Bigio tugging on his robe, taunting the old cripple.

"Let me down!"

Bigio turned to see the boy hoisted in the air, his bare feet kicking wildly above the campo stones. Pietro held the dirty collar of the boy's shirt bunched in one hand. With his other hand, he put a finger to his lips, "Quiet" he said in a loud voice. In one motion he let go of the boy and smacked him hard on the ass as he scurried away.

Pietro apologized, motioning toward the procession. He placed his hand lightly on Bigio's elbow and guided him in the opposite direction. They stopped at a small café in a campo near the hospital of the Ognissanti. Though the café was empty, Pietro glanced from side to side and looked behind him before speaking in a hushed voice.

"It wasn't Fumiani. He isn't buried in San Pantalon. I asked around. What's a friend for? I talked to Jacopo the harelip, which is never easy. Said he helped carry the body out of the church. He saw Fumiani working on the ceiling, so he knew what he looked like. The body was too large, his shoulders too broad, the hands – Fumiani's fingers were long and slender, these were thick and stubby. He knew it wasn't Fumiani, but when a priest says bury Fumiani, you bury Fumiani."

Bigio didn't say anything.

Pietro stopped, stared at him, and broke out in a wide smile, "You knew, didn't you?"

Bigio shook his head yes.

"Why didn't you tell me? Don't you trust me after all these years?"

"It isn't a question of trust. I thought you might find out some part of the truth I didn't know."

"Master Bigio, you surprise me. Did Father Zampelli know it wasn't him?"

"He says he didn't. He says he didn't want to look at the mutilated face of his friend. It was Fumiani's smock, he said."

"Do you believe him?"

"I'm not sure. If it wasn't Fumiani, there would have been a scandal. His friend was a murderer or a coward afraid for his life. Either way Zampelli would have had an even more difficult time raising the funds to finish the church. An accident was believable. It made things a lot easier for him."

"A scandal. That explains the quick burial. Something to hide." Pietro's eyes sparkled with the possibilities. "That makes it interesting, doesn't it? A good tale. Who doesn't like a good tale?"

Bigio told Pietro what he knew of Fumiani's second life on the Giudecca. He could see the wheels of intrigue and conspiracy turning in Pietro's mind. "I don't know about this Zampelli," Pietro said. "If he knew it wasn't Fumiani, it's hard to believe that he acted alone to keep it all quiet. Jacopo tells me the ceiling was cursed. Bricks and scaffolding falling to the floor, timbers lost in a fire in the warehouse. A workman twisted his ankle, stumbled, and a roll of canvas was lost in the canal. Painted panels left to dry in the courtyard ruined by the rain. They say a lazy apprentice was off pleasuring a maid in some palazzo pantry, but I don't know. Maybe someone paid him to stay away."

Sagredo, Pietro, Venetians high and low saw conspiracy in every random act. Forget the lion, Bigio thought, better a spider on the Republic's escutcheon weaving its web in thin air.

Pietro paused and his usual smile disappeared. "Be careful."

"You're the one to be careful. I'm an old man. Death's tugging at my cloak. I've one foot in Charon's boat already. You have a wife and child."

Pietro laughed, "Master Bigio, no dark thoughts. I expect you at my side when my son is baptized. If you eat my fruit, you'll live to be a hundred." He patted Bigio on his shoulder. "This Fumiani business may be layered as an onion. I'll do a bit more peeling."

Pietro, you should know your vegetables, Bigio said to himself. Keep peeling an onion and there is nothing there.

19

Bigio and Pietro returned to a quiet Campo San Barnaba. The seekers of justice still crowded the gallows in San Marco. Bigio said he didn't need looking after, but Pietro accompanied him back to the steps of the palazzo. A cat lazed across the bottom step. Pietro poked it with his boot. It didn't scamper off. The cat's head was bent at a sharp angle, its neck broken. Bigio looked up instinctively thinking the cat had lost its ninth and final life falling from the steep roof, but there were no broken tiles scattered by the stairs. Bigio saw his shutters were open. He was sure he closed them before going out. Pietro thought it an accident and kicked the cat off the step.

During Carnival there were men who would tie a cat to a board and beat it to death with their hands for sport in campo Santa Maria Formosa. What kind of men took pleasure in that or crowded San Marco to see live pigs shot from a cannon for Carnival entertainment? Perhaps the same ones who thought it more persuasive to send dark warnings not with pen and ink but the twist of a cat's neck. First, the masked shadow that followed him about and now this crude threat. It was too late. He had already disturbed a hornet's nest. The hornets were buzzing, and it wasn't simply about the death of a painter, regardless of his skill and reputation. A patrician, even a poor one, wasn't threatened so boldly over a painted ceiling.

❖

Bigio stood looking at the open birdcage. Saint Jude was gone. The journals and clothes in Fumiani's chest were undisturbed. Had his companion flown out the open window or had he been tossed out in some cruel joke? Bigio would miss his mute companionship. A good listener was as rare as an honest man in the Great Council.

Bigio slapped the empty cage. It swung back and forth, a desolate metronome to his anger. No matter his frayed cloak, he was still a patrician. Some base coward had invaded his life and dishonored his home, no matter how sparse and grim. An arrogant intruder thought he could come uninvited into his room without consequence. Bigio took on Zampelli's request out of loyalty to the priest for what he had done for his family. He did it for the family of the unknown man buried in San Pantalon. Now it was personal.

20

Carla's gloved hand trembled as she offered Bigio a small plate of almond cookies. It wasn't the fluttering hand of a coquette but the unwelcome omen of old age's final curse.

"Stefano, you surprise me. You've never spoken so freely about art."

The painting in San Benedetto had made an impression. Not Fumiani's, Bigio dismissed it as pretty but dull. It was a painting of Saint Sebastian that stopped him on his way out of the church. He didn't know the name of the artist. It wasn't the usual painting of the saint bound to a tree, his body pierced with arrows. Here a group of women, their faces lined by life, bent over the holy martyr, washing his wounds with hands rough from life's labor.

"I wanted to place a comforting hand on their draped shoulders. I wanted to reach out and pull the last arrow from Sebastian's side. There was more saintliness in the faces of these ordinary women than in the saccharine holiness of Fumiani's saints and angels." Bigio paused, "Why are you smiling? Are you making fun of me?"

"No, I'm proud of you. Looking at the world with fresh eyes. I too saw your poor Fumiani this week. I went to San Pantalon on Monday. I looked up until my shoulders ached, and I grew dizzy. Blessed Saint Pantalon, the tortures he endured. The grace of our Savior brought me to tears. I felt as if I were ascending into heaven. Poor Fumiani, a genius of the brush, a man of such faith. What more could he have done?"

Bigio paused for a moment, "It wasn't Fumiani."

Carla covered her mouth with her hand. She looked confused. "I don't understand. He didn't paint the ceiling?"

"It was his hand, but the body…that wasn't him." Bigio told Carla what he knew about Fumiani's two deaths and Zampelli's claim that he didn't look at the face because he knew from the paint splattered boots and smock that it was Fumiani. How Fumiani had fled the city and then made his way back to the Giudecca.

"Why did he come back from Padua?' she wondered.

"Maybe he missed the light," Bigio said. His answer surprised him. Before looking into Fumiani's deaths, he couldn't ever imagine seeing the world through an artist's eyes. He didn't want to worry Clara and didn't mention Sagredo by name and left out Pietro, the masked spy, the warning left at his door, the empty birdcage.

She pursed her lips and shook her head in disbelief. "You need to talk to Zampelli. He isn't telling you all he knows. What do you think happened?"

"I'm not sure. At first I believed him, now I have my doubts. But you, a woman of faith, not to believe the word of a priest?"

"Stefano, I have entertained many men of the church. They laid with me and lied to God. Why wouldn't they lie to you? Lies breed lies."

"I never lied to you nor you to me," Bigio smiled. Carla heard the irony in his voice and smiled.

"Of course, my dear Stefano, never with you. Only the others. You know lies are the flowers of a courtesan's bed. They bloom in every season. You know we lie, and we know you know. I'm not ashamed to say that I lied. But whatever was told to me in this room, I held close to my breast and shared with no one. Some of my sisters were liars of a different order. They were paid by those in the Palace to pass on what was said in their bed." Her cheeks reddened. "I never spied for the Council." She picked up a cookie between her gloved fingers. She paused, lost in the past. "Stefano, you were blinded by passion and never saw them. Spies loitered outside my steps, watching the comings and goings of those who took pleasure here. Who came here and what they did or said was no one's affair but mine. I was no party to blackmail." She reached out and held Bigio's hand. The two lovers sat in silence.

"Stefano, tell me more about this mystery you are trying to unravel."

"Some people think the dead man was murdered, maybe a case of mistaken identity."

"Why would anyone want to kill a sweet painter of such beauty?"

"I don't know."

"And you may never know. You men want to explain everything. You think there's a reason for everything. You weave intricate webs and get caught in them. Maybe you're right, maybe it was an accident. Accidents happen. There are mysteries in the world that only God understands. Stefano, don't raise your eyebrows like that. It's not becoming for a gentleman."

Bigio apologized for his rudeness and quietly ate his cookie and sipped the lukewarm coffee. He didn't want to spoil their one evening together by arguing. Yes, accidents can happen. A man can lose his balance and fall from a scaffold. But running away from your life was no accident.

21

"You knew it wasn't Fumiani, didn't you?"

Zampelli's cheeks reddened. He tugged at the wattles beneath his chin. The priest pointed to the ledge below the middle of the three windows high on the right side of the nave. "He must have struck his head on the cornice before he hit the floor. His face was smashed, all blood and pulpy flesh. He was wearing his smock, but I knew it wasn't him. He was too stocky, too short to be Giovanni. Fumiani was gone. He wasn't in the church or in his studio. His wife thought he was at the church painting late. It would have been a scandal. My friend Giovanni, a murderer? I should have told you. I am ashamed for what I did. I have confessed my sin."

"If you knew it wasn't Fumiani, why do you want me to dig up the dead?"

"Once he died on the Giudecca, I was sure he wasn't a murderer. A murderer wouldn't return to the scene of the crime. It's my duty to find out what happened in the church four years ago and why my friend disappeared."

Zampelli spoke of loyalty to a friend. Bigio wondered silently if it wasn't guilt that drove Zampelli to disturb the dead. Guilt anguished the soul more deeply than words could erase. The priest confessed his lie but needed to atone for believing his friend a murderer, for keeping the truth from Fumiani's wife, and leaving a family in the purgatory of ignorance and grief. Bigio would uncover the truth for the sake of the man lying unnamed in San Pantalon and for those who wondered what had become of the man they loved, not because he wanted to ease the priest's burden. Bigio would do it because he didn't like people who came into his room uninvited, callous people who twisted the necks of cats and tossed an innocent sparrow out among the feral cats of the city.

Zampelli brushed a tear from his eye, "Stefano, please forgive me for lying."

"If you set lies in my path, I'll never find the truth."

Zampelli tugged again on his wattle and promised he wouldn't.

Bigio told Zampelli of Sagredo's theory that perhaps someone out to kill or frighten Fumiani mistook a worker for him. "Sagredo is a man of refined sensibilities, but he lives in the past...the distant past. This is a city drunk on conspiracies. Stefano, don't follow Sagredo down some twisted path that will only lead you astray."

"If Fumiani wasn't a murderer, and nothing I've learned makes me believe he was, and if Fumiani wasn't frightened, then why did he disappear? I can't answer that question without first finding out who the dead man buried in the church is."

Zampelli shook his head, "Workers come and go, men good with a brush or hammer, men willing to work on the cheap, men running away from some sadness or failure. Men no one in Venice would miss. A man falling from a scaffold was a bad omen. The few men helping Fumiani disappeared before I could talk to them. The apprentices that ground his paints and primed his canvases were no help. They only knew the workers at the church by their nicknames. Fumiani's widow gave me the ledger he kept. I think I still have it. I will send it along to you. But I don't think it will be of much help. He only used initials and first names to mark those he paid."

Before leaving the church Bigio stopped at the entrance and looked back down the nave towards Saint Pantalon rising amidst angels into heaven's embrace. Bigio was not one of the unlettered that had to feel before they believed, but he too was moved by the dance of angels and the luminous radiance of heaven. There was joy in the tumult of their winged bodies, in the promise of faith's heavenly reward. For a moment Bigio thought there might be hope for him however faint. He floated through life, neither saint nor sinner. Like most men he did neither little harm nor little good. If he could solve the mystery of Fumiani's deaths and disappearance, he could prove to himself that his life wasn't a vain indulgence – that he was a man of honor by act and not simply by birth. He could stand before St. Peter with his head held high. He imagined Saint Peter bending over his book, straining to find marks in either column. Don't tell me what sins you haven't committed, Peter would ask, tell me what good deeds you've done. I honored the dead Bigio told Saint Peter. He paused. He thought of Carla and the promise he had made. I kept my word he said.

Outside, the man in the black mask who followed him earlier stood at the landing in front of San Pantalon. He made no effort to disguise that he was waiting for Bigio. Once he caught Bigio's eye, he turned, walked across the bridge, and disappeared among the late morning crowd in Campo Santa Margherita. Did he think himself untouchable that he could so baldly threaten a patrician? Bigio thought of going after him to invite for a chat over a cup of coffee, but he didn't think the fellow would make good company.

22

Antonio Comino rolled out across the worktable the yellowed plans for San Pantalon that his father Francesco drew over two decades before. "My father was an inspired man, a brilliant man. I'm just a humble oarsman straining to get the ship into port."

Bigio liked this plain-speaking architect immediately. He looked to be in his early fifties, thick chested with muscled forearms dense with dark hair, large hands, and calloused fingers. If he had been born with this body, Bigio thought, he would be living in his father's palazzo, the sturdy link in the long chain of Bigios, surrounded by sons wealthy enough not to wish for his quick passing and grandchildren who would kiss his cheek and ask again to hear tales of his youthful adventures.

"God willing, I will finally finish what he began." Comino traced the faded blue lines of the architectural drawing with his index finger and described with pride his father's ambitious vision. The old nave had been demolished, the total orientation of the church was shifted, the old high altar was now a chapel, and the new larger high altar stood where once old houses bordering the church had been. While it took over a decade to tear down the old nave and build and roof the new one, the church was never closed to the parishioners Comino said proudly. Zampelli wouldn't allow it. His father planned the work to make sure it never happened. "They prayed amidst the hammering and plastering. Some days you would have thought all the faithful were old and infirm with their hair grey with plaster dust."

"Twenty years and it still isn't done. That's longer than it took to build Redentore." Redentore was a much more magnificent church, built from the ground up to commemorate the end of the plague of 1576. Comino swept his hand across the plans. "My father was a perfectionist. It's in the Comino blood. Life is about doing something well. To do anything else would dishonor our name."

"And Fumiani, did he share your father's dedication?"

"Even more so. He was an artist not a mechanical, and he wouldn't let anyone confuse the two. He didn't want Zampelli telling him what to paint. He would be true to the holy martyr's life and faith in his own way." Comino smiled, "Zampelli told Fumiani that he wasn't Veronese. Not yet, Fumiani said, and he wasn't joking."

"Well, maybe the richer he made the saint's life, the costlier the painting," Bigio said.

"No, that wasn't Fumiani's way. True, there were masters whose reputation far exceeded his who squeezed the last ducat from a commission to the detriment of their art, but Fumiani was a man of honor. It was standard in a painter's contract to include a requirement that the painter use pigments of the kind approved by all experts. Some painters looking for a few more ducats scrimped on quality but not Fumiani."

Comino rolled up the plans. "The longer he painted, the more demanding he became. He didn't take compliments easily. He waved away polite praise like it was a coin meant to buy his favor."

He tapped the plans on the table to underscore what he was about to say. "He went up one too many times. That's what killed him. I'm not a man to speak harshly of the dead, but I think it was God's way of saying it's done, it's as good as man can make it. Only God is the perfect creator."

Antonio, look around at your fellow Venetians. Is this the best a perfect God can do? Bigio held his tongue. For Comino, the reason for Fumiani's fall was the fall of man himself, the presumption to think he could achieve the perfection that only God could attain. If God struck down all the presumptuous people of the city, only small children, old nuns, and pigeons would be left. For Bigio, there was no divine meaning in the mangled body on the floor of San Pantalon.

"I've heard that there were a lot of accidents while Fumiani was working on the painting. Suspicious fires, falling scaffolding."

"Accidents happen all the time," Comino said. "The delays bothered Fumiani and my father, but I don't remember either one raising any suspicions. They saved their complaints for Zampelli who was always crying poverty. Sometimes my father paid the workmen out of his own pocket to keep them happy and working until he could squeeze another handful of ducats from Zampelli."

"This is not a parish of beggars. One or two ambitious patricians could have paid for the rebuilding and gotten praise for it," Bigio said.

"True, there is no shortage of ambitious men in the Republic. But you know as well as I that a patrician mustn't seek an office or display his ambition too boldly. That was the reality Zampelli faced. No wealthy patrician in the parish wanted to pay for the renovation alone and appear as if he were buying favor for political gain in the Great Council. Zampelli was forced to get the money for the new church, almost sixty thousand ducats, year after year in small amounts from the parishioners."

Comino shook his head and let out a deep rumbling laugh. "I saw him throw his hands in the air like a tenor on the stage of San Cassiano, asking my father where he was going to find the money to knock down the houses and buy the stones, marble, and timbers to bring his vision to life. Zampelli worked hard. Smiling, tugging on sleeves, asking for another few ducats from a merchant, sweet talking a rich widow. No one could complain he was a sloth. Getting the money from him was another matter. He held coins so tightly that his knuckles turned white. If I didn't know Zampelli better, I would have thought the church wasn't his only mistress."

Patrician families with too many daughters and not enough money for a decent dowry deposited their young daughters in convents where they lived comfortably attended by their servants as if they were still back in their father's palazzo. Many entertained the wealthy and well-bred from Venice and abroad, indulging in bacchanalia and license that would shame the common prostitutes of Castelletto. No priestly sin would surprise Bigio, but he couldn't imagine Zampelli waddling through convent doors, tossing aside his cloak and cassock to lay spread-eagled like a plump putto on a young nun's bed. If Zampelli fell into sin, it would be gluttony not lust.

Every few years, when there were too many bastards born and infants buried behind convent walls or wives humiliated by their husbands' flagrant liaisons, the Great Council fulminated against the decline of morals and banished a mother superior turned brothel madam. The daughters kept coming, and after a while the hidden licentiousness grew again more brazen. Though his exploits were a century old, Bigio remembered as a boy hearing about a friar, Priapus himself with cassock and crucifix, who was roasted in San Marco for getting fifteen nuns with child in one year.

Comino was a good man. Bigio didn't want to tell him the truth about Fumiani. If Pietro was right that people in the Palace were worried about Bigio's activities, he didn't need someone else asking questions adding to their suspicions. Bigio worried that he might have already steered the hornets in Pietro's direction. He didn't want the masked shadow threatening an honorable man like Antonio Comino. Bigio didn't want an innocent man harmed because of him.

Comino was in Treviso finishing an altar and regretted he didn't make it back in time for Fumiani's funeral. He never paid him the respect he was owed, the respect his greatness deserved. The church was Comino's second home. Sometimes he was so absorbed in the demands of his daily work that he forgot to look up, or if he looked up, he didn't see.

"Looking and seeing aren't the same thing," he said. "I have to stop myself and pay attention. When you see the suffering of Pantalon and the healing grace of God, how can you not be moved? Fumiani's cheeks must have been bathed in tears every time he picked up his brush."

Comino looked up at the low ceiling and dark beams of his studio, lost for a moment in Fumiani's heaven. "Sleep well Giovanni, you are immortal."

23

The boy who delivered Bigio's note to Nicola Cassana returned empty handed. Bigio asked to talk to the painter about Fumiani as some matters had arisen that he might help in resolving. Cassana read the note and waved the boy away as if he were a bothersome mosquito. Bigio sent the boy back with another note, more honeyed than the first. Three days later Cassana wrote he could spare only few moments from his busy schedule. The Queen of England had summoned him to London to paint her portrait, and there was much to do on behalf of the Grand Prince before his departure. He agreed to meet Bigio the next afternoon in San Marco, though he doubted he could be of assistance in any matters relating to a dead artist of such minor importance.

Bigio easily spotted Cassana. He was wearing a brocaded doublet with pearl buttons, an embroidered cream-colored silk scarf pinned with an ivory cameo, and a gold embroidered black cloth cap with a gold threaded tassel. If it were not the fripperies fit for a clown or a Carnival mountebank, the small, fluffy white dog with crimson ribbon and belled collar he cradled in his lap would have given him away. Cassana remained seated and didn't extend his hand when Bigio walked over to the table to introduce himself. Despite the Republic's prohibition against this French fashion, he wore a periwig parted in the middle whose cascade of brown ringlets flowed midway down his back. His smooth cheeks were lightly rouged, and he smelt strongly of lavender. He nodded his head slightly and motioned for Bigio to sit down. Even this gesture was done with reluctance, as if it took an unbearable expenditure of energy.

A waiter headed toward the table but turned away as Cassana launched into an animated reply to a question Bigio hadn't asked. He spoke without looking at Bigio, his gaze fixed somewhere in the distant sky above the piazza.

"The price was fair. The Prince acted out of kindness for his widow's situation. There was little of value in his studio – some clay figures, a marble torso or two, sculpted hands and feet, a drawer or two of drawings. The ones by his hand, pedestrian at best. The only ones of value were those done by his masters in Bologna and his betters here. Oh yes, and there were stacks of bound journals, dusty and mildewed, full of scribbles and dull figures, the price for canvas and pots of paint, and pages and pages of his ramblings on this and that. Who cares what he thought of artists more talented than himself. I bought everything on the Prince's instructions. Whatever you might have heard otherwise are scurrilous rumors spread by jealous men whom I won't even honor by the name artist. They can only dip their pens in poison. If any of them had a good eye, they would have the ear of the Prince."

He took a perfumed silk handkerchief crisscrossed with gold threads from his doublet and patted his moist forehead and flushed cheeks. His voice rose, his right hand sliced the air, and the handkerchief fluttered above the table. The dog on his lap grew agitated. Cassana called out to the waiter to bring another chair and be quick about it. He lifted the dog onto the chair and, leaning over, patted her head, *«Princesse, calmez-vous. Nous allons bientôt partir. Il s'agit d'une peine, n'est-ce pas mon cher.»*

Like most patricians Bigio had a French tutor when he was young. He was offended less by what Cassana said than by him not speaking his own tongue among his own people. The waiter turned to get their coffees. Cassana snapped his napkin at the waiter's leg, "Don't forget the *zaletti* like you did last time and make sure they're fresh."

Bigio sipped his coffee and struggled to hide his distaste for this popinjay, who picked on his inferiors and used his tongue like a coward against a legion of imagined enemies jealous of his good fortune. To think Cassana was a man wracked by a guilty conscience would be to credit him with a conscience and the capacity for remorse. Maybe the Grand Prince did buy the contents of Fumiani's studio, more likely Cassana in the Prince's name bought it cheap for himself, then sold what he could at a steep price, keeping the models to help train the young assistants he hired to churn out fakes for the tourist trade.

"The journals, what happened to them?"

"Burned, I think. Told one of my boys to get rid of them. They were just taking up space." Cassana caught himself, "The Grand Prince has no use for such things."

Cassana ruffled his dog's head and tinkled the bells on the collar with his fingers. "The Grand Prince is a generous man. He was distressed. Fumiani left his wife little. He overpaid to ease her plight. I'm not one to slander the dead, but her husband's body was barely cold when she sought out the Prince's assistance. She didn't seem the grieving widow. She was a beauty, even in her later years. Oh how she fawned over me with sweetmeats and sweet glances. It was common talk that her appetite for fine clothes was insatiable. Everyone knew her purse was always empty. Fumiani would have finished that ceiling of his years before, if he didn't have to work to keep her in the latest fashions. Poor Fumiani tried to please God and his wife – God was easier." Cassana chuckled at his wit. "Is there anything else?"

"That's not what I wanted to talk about," Bigio said firmly, looking straight at Cassana. "It's the ceiling and his death that interest me."

Cassana smirked with undisguised self-satisfaction and tipped his head back like a man who has just won against the odds at the Ridotto. "So they're going to finally dig him up and throw his bones in the sea?"

"What do you mean?"

Cassana leaned forward and spoke with a theatrical whisper, "It wasn't an accident."

"He was murdered?"

"Who would want that mediocre fellow murdered? No, he killed himself." Cassana broke off a bit of *zaletto* and held it toward the dog who snapped it from his fingers. "The ceiling, have you looked at it? Where is the *sprezzatura*? The ease, the unstudied casualness of a true artist? Over and over he touched and retouched until he squeezed the life out of everything. He was a pedantic illustrator for the unlettered. This happened, then that happened. A player of notes but no melody."

This was a man who took pleasure in wagging his poisonous tongue, but Bigio let him carry on.

"Oh, some of his smaller works have lightness and charm, but on the big stage he has no voice of his own. He didn't paint with a singular brush. Gondoliers who shout themselves hoarse at the basest spectacle at the opera house may be awed into silence – their kind are easily impressed. It's one effect after the other but no drama, no spiritual revelation. Fumes but no fire." Cassana smiled at what he thought was a witty play on the dead man's name.

Bigio didn't have to be an uncritical enthusiast like Sagredo to consider Cassana's words a harsh judgment and a disdainful dismissal of everyone who stood in the nave of San Pantalon in awe of the heavenly scene above them. He saw no gain in debating the ceiling's spiritual power with Cassana, who would lump him among the unschooled with a flick of his hand. "I don't understand. Are you saying he killed himself because he was mediocre?"

"Mediocre and a failure and he knew it. How long had he worked on that ceiling, twenty years? It was finally done, and he looked at it and realized it was a failure and he was a failure. He finally saw himself clearly for the mediocrity he was. So then and there he crossed himself and stepped into the void. I am a blunt and honest man so forgive me if he was a friend."

"I never met the man."

Cassana had much to do before he left for England. *"Venez princesse, le temps de rentrer à la maison.»* He picked up the dog and kissed her softly on her nose before unwinding her leash and gently depositing her on the ground. "A gift from the Grand Prince. I may have to leave her with my daughter which saddens me greatly."

Bigio fingered the false stones in the pocket of his cloak. Take the dog with you. At least you will have someone to talk to who won't find an excuse to cut short the conversation and move on. "If you thought Fumiani so lacking in skill, why did the Prince commission paintings from him?"

The dog pulled on his leash. *"Maintenant, maintenant, cheri.* I didn't say he lacked skill. He lacked inspiration, the singular spark that turns a craftsman into an artist. Diligence is not enough. He was adept at architectural detail. The Prince quite admired his bizarre constructions of columns, capitals, and cornices. The architectural fancy, that was what the Prince wanted. Fumiani, unlike most *quadaraturista*, could paint figures. The Prince told him how many he wanted, the expressions on their faces, and how to place them in the painting. Still, his figures were quite pedestrian. Stiff and decorous, no spirit, no blood flowing in their veins." He paused, an undercurrent of pride crept into his voice, "But that was not a problem. I just removed them and painted them in the way the Prince desired."

Bigio couldn't hide his surprise. "Often?"

"A painting or two.

"Did Fumiani know?

"Perhaps…no, I don't think so. You must understand the paintings were done for the Grand Prince's pleasure. I did what pleased the Prince."

Bigio understood. Whether Fumiani knew or didn't know was no matter to either Cassana or the Prince. The Prince paid Fumiani and could do what he wanted.

Bigio took the glass stone from his pocket and rolled it between his thumb and forefinger so it would catch Cassana's eye. Maybe for a moment he would be deceived and regret treating a wealthy patrician so cavalierly, or maybe he would see it was a cheap imitation and, as Bigio intended, a silent comment on what he thought of Cassana. "A man takes pride in his work," Bigio said. "He couldn't have pleased him to know that his work had been altered so drastically. And if he knew, wouldn't he have been more likely 'to step into the void' as you say?"

Cassana made a small bow and left without a word or offer to pay. For a moment Bigio thought of stopping him and telling him that it wasn't Fumiani who hurtled to the floor of San Pantalon, but he choose to keep quiet. Bigio dug into his pouch for his last few coins, money well spent, if in a fleeting moment of self-awareness and humility Cassana thought he played a hand in the suicide he firmly believed in.

24

What a foolish risk. A hotheaded youth would have more sense. He should never have let Pietro talk him into it. But Bigio knew he was to blame. He told Pietro that Cassana couldn't be trusted. He wouldn't be surprised if after all these years Fumiani's journals were stacked in some corner of Cassana's studio along with the drawings and models supposedly bought by the Prince. Pietro convinced him the journals would unlock the mystery of Fumiani's disappearance. Bigio didn't put up a fight when Pietro said they should break into the studio. If they were stopped by a patrol of the Lords of the Night, Bigio would have a hard time explaining what a lame patrician and a wild-haired seller of fruit were doing shuffling along far from their homes across the Grand Canal. Pietro said not to worry. He had done "favors" for folks in every part of the city.

Bigio, Pietro, and a disgruntled Flemish painter from the studio made their way down a dark alley behind the church of San Zulian under a quarter moon. With a few questions among mongers, merchants, and men with plenty of time on their hands Pietro found a young painter, drinking his talent away, upset with the miserly wages Cassana paid. He had no allegiance to his master, now aboard a ship to London. A few drawings pawned with the Jews in the Ghetto would be recompense for a wasted year and pay his way back to Bruges. He said a side door to the studio would be easy to pry open.

The low-beamed studio was cramped with benches and easels

for a half dozen painters. Shoulder to shoulder in the dim light that seeped in from the narrow windows high along one wall, they ground out copies of old masters to fool naïve tourists who, driving a hard bargain, thought they were stealing a masterwork from a clueless Cassana. Jars of glazes, oil, and pigment were crammed along one of two shelves that ran along one wall. Small bundles of loose drawings and etchings were stacked atop the other shelf. Terra cotta and marble arms, hands, torsos, and heads, along with a few wax hands were scattered among the jars that lay on the floor against the wall. Two wooden crates were wedged in one corner. Under flickering candlelight Bigio rummaged through the bundles and found mostly unsigned drawings of faces, torsos, hands, putti, and a few angels. Some could have been from Fumiani's hand, but it was difficult for Bigio to distinguish one artist's work from another. The young painter rolled up several drawings and put them in a rough cloth bag slung over his shoulder. Bigio went slowly along the length of the shelf but didn't find any journals. Pietro bent over a crate and pulled out a marble hand missing the tips of its fingers wrapped loosely in a sheet of paper. He waved it in the air for Bigio to see. He unwrapped a rusted dagger in a worn scabbard. He tossed the rumpled paper on the floor. He bent over to rummage through the two crates.

"Nothing, just junk," his voice muffled by the sides of the crate.

Bigio was disappointed by their futile venture and nervous that the candlelit studio would draw attention late at night. He went over to hurry Pietro along. Pietro handed him an object wrapped in paper and twine. It was a tarnished copper goblet, its lip cracked in two places. The crumbled paper in his left hand and the goblet in his right, Bigio was about to put the goblet back in the crate when he hesitated.

"The paper," he said. "Unwrap everything. Give me the paper." It was in Fumiani's hand, Bigio was sure of it. Pages torn from the journals. Arches, columns, architectural details, and on some sheets, writing. He and Pietro quickly and excitedly unwrapped the twenty or so objects in the crates. A lifetime of ideas and thoughts burned to ashes. All that was left were two dozen crumpled sheets. Bigio smoothed them out roughly on a bench, rolled them up, tied them with twine, and nestled the roll under his cloak.

The Flemish painter stood in front of a bench, unbuttoned his pants, and, smiling, pissed back and forth across the feet of the easel in front of him. Pietro laughed and did the same against the side of one of the crates. Bigio snuffed out the candles with his fingers, and they left the studio.

❖

Bigio pulled the sheets of rough paper back and forth across the edge of his table to smooth out the wrinkles. Few sheets had dates or had been torn out so roughly from the journals that the dates were missing or impossible to make out. Most of the sheets were pencil drawings of architectural details and angels viewed from below. Fumiani was a man obsessed with heaven. What little writing there was, was dull and inconsequential: pigments bought, haggling over lumber and canvas, comments on the effects of unseasonable wet weather, and the coming and going of apprentices. There were no windows onto Fumiani's soul for Bigio to peer through. One sheet seemed odd. Just one sentence at the top of the page, then crossed out: "Laura, I want to tell you about my day." Was Fumiani traveling and drafting a letter to his wife? If he were in Venice, why would he write when he could speak to her across the dining table or when his head lay next to hers on the pillow at night?

Only one other sheet held any interest for Bigio. It told a charming tale unknown to him that Carla might find touching. Bigio only knew it was an episode from the life of Fra Filippo Lippi because Fumiani had written "Vasari – Fra Filippo Lippi" at the top of the sheet. Fumiani copied it word for word and underlined the last line:

Now, chancing to be in the Marches of Ancona, he was dis-
porting himself one day with some of his friends in a little
boat on the sea, when they were all captured together by the
Moorish galleys that were scouring those parts, and taken to
Barbary, where each of them was put in chains and held as
a slave; and thus he remained in great misery for eighteen
months. But one day, seeing that he was thrown much into
contact with his master, there came to him the opportunity
and the whim to make a portrait of him; whereupon, taking
a piece of dead coal from the fire, with this he portrayed
him at full length on a white wall in his Moorish costume.
When this was reported by the other slaves to the master
(for it appeared a miracle to them all, since drawing and
painting were not known in these parts), it brought about
his liberation from the chains in which he had been held
for so long.

A lovely story: an artist saved by his art. A romantic notion far
from Fumiani's ordinary life trudging up and down a scaffold day
after day for twenty years.

25

Bigio had little choice. Fumiani's widow was dead. Cassana in his arrogance and self-importance destroyed whatever hints Fumiani might have left in his journals about his disappearance. All that remained was Fumiani's art: drawings from the Giudecca and paintings in the churches of the city. If Fumiani left any clues to be deciphered, they would be in his paintings. Bigio would have to do what he had not done before: pay attention to the art around him, the art he had looked at but not seen. If he understood Fumiani's art, maybe he could see the world through the artist's eyes. If he saw the world through Fumiani's eyes, then maybe, just maybe, he could decipher his soul.

Bigio had entered the Church of San Rocco a few times over the last half century for a funeral mass though he couldn't remember the names of the dead. He didn't remember what episodes from Saint Roch's life were portrayed on the church walls and ceiling nave. It was as if he were walking into the church for the first time. In the highest area of the nave vault Saint Roch, seen from below, stood atop a steep staircase clad in luxuriant cloth of red, gold, and blue surrounded by the poor, their hands outstretched in supplication. Five columns of an open courtyard towered above the saint like a theatrical backdrop. Bigio could see what impressed the young Zampelli: Fumiani's mastery of architectural detail – the columns, arches, and balustrades, the many figures set in dramatic poses, and the almost dizzying illusion that placed the faithful themselves on the steps looking up, ready to receive material blessings from Saint Roch. Substitute the emperor Maximian for Saint Roch, the emperor's jealous physicians for the poor, and open up the courtyard to the vastness of heaven, and the painting was a detail from the ceiling in San Pantalon. Bigio sensed Fumiani's bravado and self-confidence. He was an ambitious artist making a claim for attention: the sculpted bodies in motion, the play of light on the folds of fabric, the architectural elements rendered with a draughtsman's keen eye. Bigio understood how the painting's dramatic immediacy appealed to a priest new to his own church who wanted to impress his parishioners. Why should the parishioners pay to see extravagant display and splendor at the opera houses and theaters springing up in the city when they could be moved at no cost by the spectacle of the glorious apotheosis of a saint surrounded by a flurry of angels and the son of God floating in heaven above their heads?

On the left wall of the church in a luminescent pink robe and blue cloak Christ was cleansing the temple filthy with lambs, cows, and the broken cages of fowls. As profaners of the holy space scrambled and tumbled to avoid his wrath, Christ waved a rope scourge in the air, ready to bring it down on the head of a cowering man, his hands over his head to protect himself from the Savior's wrath. It was a dramatic scene well rendered, but Bigio was bothered by a figure in the right foreground, a bearded man in a white turban, his right arm raised to ward off a holy blow. To his unschooled eye the elderly man seemed a giant, out of proportion to the figures around him. For a man trained and skilled in the laws of perspective, it seemed a strange failure that diluted the immediacy of the scene.

These two paintings were the only ones Fumiani did for the church. It was Tintoretto who dominated the walls of the nave and the chancel. A Venetian of even faltering faith could no more avoid Tintoretto than a seagull could avoid the water. His ambition was legendary. Was there a tale from the Bible that he had not illustrated? This was the company Fumiani wanted to keep, this was one of the artists that Sagredo and Zampelli believed he was talented enough to hang beside.

The Tintorettos were dark, disturbing paintings. When Bigio leaned over the chancel's low marble balustrade, he felt he was standing next to Tintoretto, one foot in the looming darkness out of which the paintings emerged like the islands of the lagoon in the morning fog. Bigio once thought painters summoned their visions from some dream world that only they could enter. Tintoretto hadn't dreamt from night's dark cloth this prison cell, this lazaretto, and forest path. It was as if he had stumbled upon these scenes with brush and palette in hand. These were real plague sores, red discs of imminent death in armpits and inner thighs. These were real chains and shackles. These were the mutilated limbs of the tortured and hopeless. In the center of the prison cell a blue-robed angel haloed in divine light hovered over Saint Roch to comfort him. Bigio's eyes moved to a prisoner chained at the neck to the wall on the right and another young prisoner in the bottom of the painting, his head and severed arm stuck through the bars of a subterranean dungeon. The margins, the incidental image, the fleeting detail bore dark truths. Without the darkness the divine light would not shine as bright. Without pain and hopelessness there was no need for God's comfort and healing touch. Without death there was no resurrection.

Above this painting hung Tintoretto's dizzying, nightmare vision of Saint Roch's capture in the chaos of battle. Bigio leaned back instinctively to avoid the horses and soldiers tumbling headfirst off the canvas. A horse, a large banner trailing behind, soared through the air like a winged stallion. A regiment of soldiers dim as ghosts stood ready with pikes and swords in the spectral background. Bigio didn't feel like a distanced observer. He was a participant in the danger, death, and pain of battlefield, prison cell, and lazaretto. While Fumiani's figures were well modeled, they seemed like actors in studied poses compared to Tintoretto, who with a sorcerer's spell stopped the continuous flow of time for a frozen moment. Bigio spent more time looking at Tintoretto's paintings than Fumiani's but still felt there was more to see. He promised himself he would return once he got to the bottom of the Fumiani affair.

26

Bigio walked across the campo from the Church of San Rocco to the Scuola San Rocco to see the works Sagredo said Fumiani painted there. Every Venetian knew the tale of Tintoretto's ruse to win the commission for the Sala dell'Albergo in the Scuola. He didn't prepare a drawing of a proposed painting as was required. He snuck in the night before the selection to put a completed painting on the ceiling. For the next twenty years he painted masterworks for the Scuola's walls and ceilings. Bigio hesitated on the steps of the Scuola, afraid he might be mistaken for a poor brethren in need of bread, flour, and a cloak for the winter, or worse a beggar looking for alms. Bigio pushed aside his pride and the heavy oak door.

As a boy Bigio went with his father to the Scuola San Giovanni Evangelista to pray before the jewel-encrusted reliquary of the true cross that had been in the Scuola for over three centuries. It seemed to Bigio a small, plain sliver of wood that might have been thrown out with the wood shavings and sawdust from the floor of a cabinetmaker's shop. For the rich and powerful of the city, citizen and patrician alike, it was a holy relic that brought wealth and prominence to the Scuola. His brother had been a member of the confraternity, but Bigio hadn't set foot in San Giovanni since his death. The charity of the state was shame enough. He had vague memories of once coming to San Rocco as a boy with his family to hear a concert of sacred music on the saint's feast day, but he had no recollection of Tintoretto's paintings.

Bigio's footsteps and the tap of his cane echoed across the marble tiles of the Scuola's deserted ground floor. There were no distraught families of sailors petitioning the members to ransom their sons and husbands captured by Moorish pirates, no brethren waiting to plead the case of their young daughters in need of dowries, just Bigio, Tintoretto, and an elderly porter, bent-backed as a scythe, shuffling from behind a corner table to ask if he could be of any help.

"Fumiani?" The old man struggled to remember the name. "Oh yes, Fumiani. I've been here forty years, Bellini, Titian, and of course Master Tintoretto but Fumiani...the one who fell...not many come asking after him. Follow me." Bigio slowed down to walk by the side of the porter, whose gait was even slower than his.

"So you knew Fumiani?"

"Zanchi, Negri, Pianti, Fumiani. I knew them all." He pointed to his white hair. "I even knew Saint Roch himself...when he was a boy," he laughed at a joke he had told countless times to strangers and brethren who long let it pass without comment. "It was a long time ago, over thirty years, but I remember Fumiani. He was a serious man, more serious than the rest. Even Zanchi smiled."

At the top of the stairs, the porter turned left, walked a few steps, and stopped at the foot of another broad stairway leading up to the Sala Capitolaire. Bigio looked at the painting on his right. No wonder Fumiani didn't smile, burdened by the death and grief it was his charge to paint. A bridge filled with the plague's dead and dying, corpses carted off in the distance, and a dead body dumped into a gondola already full of bodies. On the bridge a man held his nose to block the stench of the dead lying at his feet. Bigio, staring at Fumiani's achievement, heard the cries of the living and smelled the foul odor of death.

"Zanchi was a fine painter," the old man swept his hand toward the painting. Then he pointed to the barrel vault above the stairs. "That's your Fumiani."

Bigio walked up a few steps to get a better view of the small dome about twelve feet across. Heaven in a light blue palette floated above his head. Saint Roch seen from below in foreshortened perspective was protecting or comforting a white-robed maiden kneeling before him, while an angel partially hidden in the clouds above looked on. To the saint's right a female figure rose above a pyramid of bodies, her head haloed by the light of the dove of the Holy Spirit. Bigio thought she might be Charity since a man to her right held out his hand toward her in supplication. The bland scene suffered in comparison to the emotional power of Zanchi's plague scene below.

The old man sensed Bigio's disappointment. "Not my favorite. I liked it better before they painted it over."

Bigio was confused. "This isn't Fumiani?"

"Was. But they painted it over last year. Some members complained the colors were too dark, Saint Roch too stiff. They wanted something more pleasing to the eye. Pellegrini did it. Hear he's off in England." He pointed to four muscular males crouching in the triangular spaces beneath the dome and the two female figures on the lunettes either side of the dome. "They left those. That's Fumiani's hand."

Bigio hoped Fumiani never found out that his work had lasted barely thirty years before it was thought out of fashion, too serious for these dissolute times. Bigio hoped he died thinking he and Tintoretto were bound together forever, esteemed for eternity.

Fumiani's remaining figures sat scrunched, knees drawn up, the weight of the dome bearing down on the painted capitals balanced on their heads. With muscles tensed, they clutched the folds of their cloaks and bore the heavy burden of their worlds. Bigio couldn't decipher the symbolic clues and identify the female figures. Maybe they represented Peace or Science – the porter shrugged in defeat. Bigio saw Fumiani's special ability to merge figures with architectural elements, real and illusory, within a limited space. He seemed fascinated by the possibilities of perspective and looked for any way to show off his skill, no matter how small the space or ordinary the imagery, like a young boy flexing his muscles in front of a mirror. The figures were painted to be seen from below, their robes draped over the painted ledge where they sat cross-legged. The soles of their feet gave them a humanity that their plain, inexpressive faces didn't.

"If you think they're beautiful, you should have seen his wife," the porter said, making a soft clicking sound with his tongue. "Brethren came to the Scuola just to see her. The workmen dawdled when she was around. Fumiani wasn't much concerned with appearances, shirtsleeves dusted with chalk and his fingers stained with ink and paint. She always looked like she was on her way to a Carnival ball in a fine silk dress, and never the same one. He was a considerate husband, careful never to touch her with his dirty hands." The old man rummaged among dusty memories. "She was full of praise for him. Thought him heir to the great souls – Veronese, Titian, even Tintoretto himself. That's a good wife for you."

Or a burden to bear. The bells of San Rocco marked the hour. The porter had work to do, excused himself, and invited Bigio to spend as much time as he wanted looking at the Tintorettos. "I was barely twelve when I came here. Been here over sixty years. No one has looked at these walls more than I have. Every day I feel God's presence. Every day I hear God's voice in these paintings."

Tintoretto's paintings stretched the entire length of the ceiling in elaborately carved golden frames the shape of ovals, diamonds, and rectangles. It was like standing beneath a bejeweled reliquary. Bigio walked the length of the hall and back again, leaning on his cane for balance as he looked up at each of the twenty-one paintings. Bigio was glad the porter wasn't with him so he could look at the paintings in silence. He didn't want words to get in the way.

Standing beneath the largest painting, Bigio looked up at a hillside of twisted bodies and writhing snakes and a sky full of tumbling, flying angels beneath the outstretched arms of God. His eyes were drawn upward to the miracle of the bronze serpent that Moses used to heal the repentant Jews. Bigio remembered the miracle from a long-ago homily. There was an energy, a joyful exuberance in this painting, despite the pain of writhing bodies, as if Tintoretto loved not just God's healing power but the act of painting itself. Look at my painting, Tintoretto seemed to be saying, and I will heal you.

In the center of the Sala dell'Albergo was *Saint Roch in Glory*, the artist's first commission at the Scuola, won by stealth and skill. Bigio knew he should focus on the haloed saint who God welcomed with outstretched arms. What caught his attention instead was a figure at the right edge of the painting whose severed arms looked like they had been chopped off below the elbow, just like the thief's in the painting in the church of San Rocco. If a thief could gain redemption and enter the gates of heaven to stand alongside a saint, maybe an ordinary man like himself could do the same. Maybe it was never too late to redeem oneself in the eyes of God.

Stretching the length of the wall opposite the entrance to the Sala dell'Albergo was *The Crucifixion*. Christ was bathed in light amidst a vast scene full of emotion and action where no detail was extraneous, where Tintoretto did nothing to flaunt his skill, yet his skill was powerfully clear. Bigio admired the loyal wife who believed her husband deserved a place in the pantheon of great artists and praised him beyond what more objective eyes believed his achievement merited. A wife could be forgiven. Who today could think Fumiani was Tintoretto's equal? The hardest truth to bear was to recognize your limitations, to know where you belonged. Pity the man who lived in illusion. Pity the man who believed he could reach his long-sought and well-deserved destination but one day realized he never would. That was the ultimate unhappiness.

Bigio heard the bells of San Rocco mark an hour that passed quickly as a sigh. The paintings were too powerful, too beautiful. Bigio stopped seeing. He made his way down the stairs to the ground floor. He felt both exhausted and strangely alive from all he had seen. When he stepped out into the campo, he shielded his eyes with his hand from the bright light. It was as if he was an infant, fresh from the womb, seeing the world for the first time. The white marble façade of the church of San Rocco and the red brick walls of I Frari at the end of the campo glowed in the sunlight.

27

Some days when the breeze was light under a clear, blue sky and the coffee dark and smooth, the cawing of gulls sounded like the laughter of children. Today under a heavy, gray sky it sounded like mournful wailing as Bigio walked across the campo toward San Zaccaria. Sagredo said there was a painting in the church that Fumiani had done during the last years of his life while working on the ceiling. Bigio, needing to catch his breath, sat for a few minutes on one of the broken capitals from the old church scattered in a small garden in front of the Benedictine convent next to San Zaccaria. He was tired less from the walk than feeling he was swimming against the tide, the receding water taking him further from shore, the bottom hidden beneath deep murky water. He seemed no closer than when he began to finding out who lay buried beneath the marble floor of San Pantalon and why Fumiani fled. He didn't hold out much hope that another Fumiani painting or the tombs of the half dozen doges buried in the church would give him an answer. Alive, the doges were richly clothed mummers muffled by protocol and procession. Dead, they lay silent in their marble tombs.

Young English gentlemen and well-dressed ladies on the Grand Tour clustered in front of the Bellini altarpiece. They gazed in silent reverence at Bellini's Madonna on her throne in holy conversation with Saints Jerome, Peter, Lucy, and Catherine, each serene as a statue. Bigio doubted that their guide pointed out that a Fumiani hung high up on the wall above them. After a few respectful minutes they moved on without looking up at the Fumiani. Bigio didn't blame them.

The painting commemorated the visit of Frederick II, the Holy Roman Emperor, and the Doge to the Convent of San Zaccaria over four hundred years before, a visual report of a dull scene of no interest to a contemporary Venetian. It was a competent effort without an ounce of emotional power. Bigio's eyes were drawn not to the ermine clad emperor and his regal host but to two groups of nondescript figures at the margin of the royal visitation. Two young men in the top right corner of the painting clung to columns on a narrow ledge to get a better view of the emperor. Behind them in the deep foreground was an architectural bravura of columns, arches, balcony, and balustrade. It was as if he was saying, "Let me show you what I do best," inviting the viewer to leave Frederick and the Doge and come to San Pantalon to see the true expression of his artistry. Three even more anonymous figures stood each in the same pose with their backs to the viewer, left legs thrust behind their twisted torsos. This repetition of a stock pose seemed to send the same message: my soul is not in this painting; I am doing this to pay the bills. Maybe Cassana was right. Married to a woman with an appetite for fine things and with Zampelli clutching the church's purse with a tight fist, Fumiani was forced to take on commissions to keep his wife happy. This only slowed down the completion of the ceiling that would be for him his masterpiece and for her the calling card to fame and wealth. Sometimes what we want gets in the way of what we need. That was an answer to a question, but Bigio wasn't sure it was the question he was trying to answer.

28

Carla chided Bigio for being late for his weekly visit. "When you were young and hot-blooded, you stood at my door for hours waiting for me to finish my toilette."

Anxious for her company and her bed, Bigio often came before sunset, but he never waited for hours. A patrician never waited for anyone, unless it was another patrician. If it brought her happiness to think so, Bigio wouldn't argue. She was sitting on her bedroom settee. He bent over and kissed her on the cheek. When she reached up to touch his cheek, her hand trembled more than the week before.

"I went to see Fumiani's painting in San Zaccaria."

"I don't know it. Is it a good work?"

"No, a dull affair. Not his fault. He wasn't given anything to say. No heaven to paint, no holy martyrs, just ordinary men of power posing for the crowd." Thinking its gentle holiness would appeal to Carla, Bigio described the Bellini for her. He told her of his visit to San Rocco and the power of the Tintorettos. Bigio was surprised by the emotion in his voice, the details he remembered, and the thoughts that tumbled out.

"Stefano, a dead man has opened your eyes. How wonderful. We will have to see some treasures together. We will see Veronese one day, a favorite of mine. And your bill collecting," she smiled, "how is that going?"

Bigio shared his frustration at the unanswered questions and dead ends – the destroyed journals, Zampelli's lie, and Cassana's venomous tongue. He left out Pietro's warnings, St. Jude's disappearance, and the mysterious shadow who had become an almost daily presence in his life. He didn't want to upset her. If Anna Ridolfi and Cassana were to be believed, one's memory addled by drink, the other's soul poisoned by envy and sycophancy, Fumiani's wife didn't warm his marriage bed and kept his purse perpetually empty with her social ambition and extravagance.

"Maybe you're right, maybe I'm fashioning an elaborate explanation for what was a simple accident, a convenient accident for Fumiani. The ceiling finished, he used the dead man to escape his wife and an unhappy marriage."

Carla laughed. "Pardon me, Stefano have you forgotten where you are? In Venice no man has to leave his wife to find pleasure. That is what I'm here for. There are more arms in Venice to comfort an unhappy man than jeweled treasures in San Marco. His poor wife – you men always take credit for your success and blame a woman for your failures."

Bigio stood guilty as accused. Marriage was for him the Promised Land seen only from a distance. Bigio lost his virginity with awkward fumbling in a gondola's curtained felze to a married woman, who, freed by velvet mask and festive license, took pity on a smooth-cheeked cripple she thought might never find pleasure in a marriage bed. Since then he paid for his pleasure or received it unbidden from unhappy wives at Carnival.

"Stefano, do you think that only men in this Republic have ambition? Do you think Fumiani's wife – what was her name?"

"Laura."

"Do you think Laura was the first woman who wanted her husband to succeed so she could live well? She wasn't the first woman to push a man to heights he wouldn't have climbed himself. Look at the last dogaressa. She wanted to be dogaressa more than sweet Silvestro Valiero wanted to be doge. He would have been happy to have lived the good life as an ambassador in London or Paris."

Elisabetta Querini's appetite for power and status was well known. While Silvestro had a fine figure, a handsome profile, and could make an eloquent banquet toast, it was Elisabetta who ruled the Ducal Palace. Posters plastered on the walls of the city skewered her ambition and extravagance with scurrilous wit. For a half century the law forbade the coronation of the dogaressa as a useless profligacy. It was common knowledge she pushed her husband to convince the Great Council to disregard the law. Bigio remembered the excessive decoration in the Ducal Palace she ordered erected to celebrate her ascension. Every guild in the Republic from painters and silversmiths to silk weavers and mirror makers was assigned a room or corridor where they were commanded to build a booth in honor of the dogaressa. One couldn't say no to the Querinis and the Valieros. He remembered with disgust the triumphal arch in praise of the noble lineages of doge and dogaressa at the entrance to the office of Foreign Affairs: angels crowned Elisabetta while Piety, Modesty, and other Virtues stood shamefaced around her. Pity the poor painters charged with such hypocrisy. Other dogaressas were content to rule their parlor maids and kitchen cooks. Elisabetta Querini sat on the throne wearing the jeweled Ducal crown, a sable-trimmed robe of gold cloth, a mantle embroidered in gold with silver embossed flowers, and a necklace with a diamond cross, and received with unseemly pomp foreign ambassadors, bishops, patriarchs, the Papal Nuncio, and the highest officials of the Republic. Rumor was, her poor put-upon husband died of apoplexy during an argument with his domineering wife over her meddling in affairs of state. How far she exceeded the bounds of her position was clear after Silvestro's death. The Great Council once again forbade the wasteful coronation of the dogaressa. No future dogaressa could wear the ducal crown or receive the envoys of foreign powers and high officials of the Republic, excessive retinues were forbidden, and the dogaressa could leave the Palace attended only by members of her close family and a few private attendants.

"Did you ever see her?" Bigio asked scornfully.

"Now Stefano be a gentleman. Remember she was a woman in her sixties when she became dogaressa."

Age wasn't the culprit. She was never an attractive woman. She struck a medal to commemorate her coronation with a flattering portrait of pure imagination. She had a thin face, long nose, a high forehead, and a pursed mouth. She looked as if she were weaned on a lemon.

"I wasn't thinking of the face God gave her. It was her prideful scowl, her bearing of disdain toward everyone, even the patricians in the Great Council. She acted as if she were a queen blessed by blood rather than the wife of a Republic's leader elected by free men."

"Calm yourself, Stefano. Don't let the dead disturb you so."

Carla was right. There was no reason to let an empty sack of a man and a haughty woman wrinkled as a prune upset him. Whatever went on in the Ducal Palace didn't put more polenta on his table or stop the weeds from growing under the eaves and clogging the rainspout above his window. The Querinis traced their line back to the Roman nobles who fled to the lagoon to escape the Huns and Lombards at the very beginning of the Republic's history. Elisabetta counted among her ancestors generals, scholars, and holders of high office. Silvestro's father may have been a doge, and the Valieros one of the old families of the Republic, but Elisabetta Querini thought she was marrying down. Her overweening pride and profligacy insulted Bigio. The war with the Turks left the city's coffers bare, but she and Silvestro continued to host banquets and balls as if it were the halcyon days of the Republic. Bejeweled in cloth of gold and silver, a diamond cross hanging against her flat chest, she was a glittering insult to the saints and martyrs of the faith and the struggling citizens of the Republic. Bigio admired those who sought power out of principle and high purpose, unlike Elisabetta Querini, who was driven by love of luxury and a blinkered sense of entitlement.

She died last year, nine years after Silvestro. It was a waste of anger and time thinking about them. They were symptoms of the Republic's decline. They had nothing to do with an anonymous man's death and a painter's disappearance. Talking about them would only spoil his one night with Carla. It was time to forget the follies of a weak man moldering in his tomb and his prodigal wife. Time to forget his tired body, bad stomach, and the mystery of Fumiani. It was time to summon the past. Time to remember his fingers tracing circles on Carla's perfumed breasts.

The light was fading when Bigio left Carla. For the first time the masked man followed him there and was loitering a few steps from her door. Carla might be flattered that someone still thought her a courtesan with clients worth spying on. Bigio knew this was no ordinary spy doing the Council's business. This wasn't a spy sent to report on his amorous proclivities. This was a messenger sent to warn him that he was asking too many questions, that it was time to go back to his room, to bury himself in the ancient histories of Pliny and Polybius. If he didn't, innocent people would suffer. Bigio heard the man laugh before he turned and walked away. Bigio wished in that moment that his cane was a rapier. He would put its tip against the man's throat and demand to know who sent him and why. He would run him through and whoever sent him without a second thought if he caused Carla any harm – if he even crossed her threshold with his dirty boots. He promised Carla he would save her from destitution and beggary. Now he silently promised her his life to protect her.

29

Bigio closed the shutter and window to keep out the damp evening air. One of Fumiani's rough spun cotton shirts hung over the back of the chair pushed against the table in the middle of the room. Bigio took to draping it over his shoulders to keep out the evening chill. Carla would think it morbid, if not sacrilegious, to wear a dead man's clothes. In some strange way he couldn't explain, Bigio thought if he wore the shirt, he might come closer to understanding the mystery of the man.

The candle cast a circle of light in the middle of the table. Bigio pushed Vasari's *Lives of the Most Excellent Italian Painters, Sculptors, and Architects, from Cimabue to Our Times* to the far corner of the table. The week before Sagredo sent over the thick leather bound book with the simple note, "Look up." Bigio was touched that Sagredo thought him capable of becoming a more cultured man at his age. Every day he read a few of the biographies. Raphael, Michelangelo, Botticelli, Donatello, Alberti, the Bellinis, and Titian were artists that any educated man who breathed the air of Italy knew. There were many other artists known only to a Florentine, and then only to those of artistic learning. He wondered if it was his ignorance alone that made Cavallini, Barna da Siena, Spinello Aretino, and Ercole Ferrarese, among many others, as foreign to him as the rulers of ancient Babylonia, or were most artists swallowed by the ravening maw of time?

Bigio laid the sheet of paper flat on the table and put two spoons and two cups on the corners to keep the edges from curling.

Bigio looked once again at the gentle face that he had thought was the Virgin Mary when he first encountered it among the papers in Fumiani's rooms. Now that he was paying attention to the Republic's Annunciations and Madonnas, he wasn't so sure. She didn't have the surprised modesty of the Virgin in the presence of Gabriel flying across the threshold or the caring calmness of the Madonna looking down at the plump Christ child on her lap. Her eyes stared out at him, open and alluring, her lips ready to be kissed.

Bigio flipped through the pages of one of the journals brought over from the Giudecca, looking for her. He found a profile from the right at the top of a page filled with angels and putti, her profile from the left on another. On some pages there were just her lips and chin, forehead crowned with ringlets. In the corner of a sheet filled with arches, dentils, and capitals he found her long aquiline nose. Fumiani's hand returned to her again and again. He caressed this woman with pen and brush. Not the woman as she was when he fled, but as she was when he first fell in love with her. This was not a man who abandoned a wife he no longer loved.

Amidst the floating angels and putti, Bigio noticed a figure shorn of angel's wings that tumbled down the margins of several pages. In some of the drawings he plunged feet first toward the unseen earth, his long hair streaming above him. In another he hurtled head down, his hands clawing the air, his eyes wide in disbelief. In one drawing he was open mouthed, asking a question there was no time to answer. Angels and putti were cut from the same cloth, interchangeable one with the other. This falling man was unique: thick eyebrows, wide forehead, a bent nose broken perhaps in an accident or fight, muscled arms, and the veined hands of a workman.

Did Fumiani watch the dead man fall from the scaffold? Or did he come upon the body splayed on the marble floor, his head pooled in red, and imagine his last seconds as he hurtled to his death? If love returned him over and over to memories of his young wife, what drew his hand like a magnet to a body falling to its death? The horror of watching helpless as the body plummeted from the scaffold? Or did guilt prick his pen? Guilt over what?

30

Zampelli found Fumiani's ledger and sent it over to Bigio. A dry enumeration of materials bought and workmen paid, it didn't go as far back as Bigio expected. Fumiani kept careful records in a neat hand: monies from Zampelli, the cost of canvas, brushes, paper, chalk, pigment, ink, linseed oil, wood for armature and scaffolding, and payments to carpenters, apprentices, and bargemen. He wrote the full names of some of the workers and for others just their first name or nickname. The carpenters and the boatmen who moved canvas from studio to church were Venetians who would have been missed and whose family names Pietro likely knew. The helpers at the church were itinerant craftsmen, whose first names were all they wanted Fumiani to know. Bigio wrote down the names of everyone without a family name that Fumiani paid the year before his "death." He asked Pietro to find out if the laborers working on the church knew any of them.

Bigio met Zampelli in a café near the church to talk about the ledger and the financing of the ceiling.

"I paid Fumiani what he asked for," Zampelli paused, "when I had the money. Raising funds wasn't easy. The war with the Ottomans cost us dearly. Ships sat at the docks, their holds empty. You could hear orphaned coins clinking sadly in my parishioners' pockets and purses."

"Why," Bigio wondered, "were payments spread out more over the last year of the painting than in the years before, even during the hard times of the war years?"

Zampelli paused, searching for an answer. He pulled on his wattles. "I don't remember. Maybe things were slowing down and Giovanni didn't need so much. I don't really remember." Zampelli stammered and wiped his forehead with his hand.

Fumiani worked on the ceiling for twenty years, but the ledger only started in 1690. "Where," Bigio wanted to know, "were the earlier ledgers?"

Zampelli leaned forward and spoke firmly, visibly more comfortable with this question. "After Father Vinanti died and I came to San Pantalon in '75, I gave Giovanni my word that he would paint the ceiling. No contract, just my word. We didn't sign a contract until almost ten years later. There was no money, and the old church hadn't been torn down. The old nave came down in '82, and we didn't lay the new foundation until the end of '84. In '84 people were still living in buildings where the high altar is now. We tore them down when we shifted the nave. We didn't roof the new nave until '90. How could you paint a ceiling for a building without a roof? And once we put up the roof, we still had to raise money for the ceiling. Those were trying times." He rubbed his chin and pulled once more on his wattles. "Giovanni may have thought about the ceiling for twenty years and done sketches, but if he did, it was on his own initiative with no contract or money from me."

"What about all the talk about the painting taking twenty years?"

"Stefano, a myth, an heroic fabulation. Veronese worked in San Sebastiano for twenty years, Tintoretto twenty years in San Rocco. Twenty years put him in the company of the gods. Fumiani never bragged how long he sketched and thought about the ceiling, that wasn't his temperament. Laura, saintly wife that she was, wasn't shy about claiming the mantle of greatness for her husband, especially after he died. This was his San Rocco, his San Sebastiano. After she died, it made for a story that pulled at the heartstrings, and I must say the purse strings. I admit I haven't raised my voice to correct the myth. I still need money to finish the church. There are chapels to complete. The façade is still brick. Comino's marble façade will cost a great deal, but raising the money should be easier now."

"Why easier now?"

"Oh, just less demands," he said with a faint smile as if savoring a private joke.

Bigio wondered how he would uncover the truth about Fumiani when, even while the paint was still wet, his life was barnacled in myth. How much of the past do we really know, when what happened in our own lifetime was cocooned in myth and misunderstanding?

"Even if I could have raised the money more quickly, I don't think the ceiling would have been finished any quicker. Dear Giovanni was such a perfectionist. He worked deliberately and did almost all the painting himself."

"But he had assistants," Bigio said.

"An assistant might copy a small vase, garland, or bit of ornamentation, and once in a rare while near the end touch up a figure or an architectural element. I saw detailed preliminary drawings in his studio, but I never saw any of his assistants paint from the drawings either there or in the church."

Zampelli paused and said again, "Yes, a perfectionist." He shook his head to add emphasis to his double declaration.

Bigio picked up the ledger from the table without saying anything. Zampelli wasn't trying to convince him as much as he was trying to convince himself that Fumiani, not the lack of money, was the reason the ceiling took so long.

31

Pietro relished the intrigue of the investigation. He chose to meet in the treasury of the Basilica, hiding in plain sight among foreign pilgrims crowded in silent awe in front of a fragment of the true Cross, the leg bone of Saint Simon, the thigh bone of Saint Ursula, the arm of Saint Luke, thorns from the Savior's crown, and the very blood of Christ. Bigio knew it didn't matter where they met if he and Pietro had drawn the attention of the Council of Ten.

Two portly French priests jostled Pietro to get a better look at the silver gilded cone that contained the arm of Saint Pantalon. Bigio was afraid Pietro would curse their maternal lineage, but he held his tongue. "These rude pilgrims are good for business," Pietro whispered. Pilgrims spent money. Venetians praised the good Christians of the Republic who delayed ships to the Holy Land for "special repairs" to keep the foreign faithful expensively accommodated and their purses open for a few extra days.

Bigio hadn't seen Pantalon's reliquary since his mother brought him here as a young boy. The silver reliquary had rested in San Marco for over five hundred years after the triumphal capture of Constantinople. It was enameled with episodes from the saint's life and martyrdom. Its base of tendrils and leaves was embedded with precious stones.

"What do you think? Is that really his arm in there?" Pietro asked.

"The man of faith in me wants to believe it is. But I am a Venetian. I have my doubts."

"Have you lost your faith?"

"In miracles."

Bigio and Pietro walked out of the treasury toward the quieter north entrance of San Marco. They passed the tombs of doges and the bays whose glittering mosaic domes depicted the Biblical tales of creation, flood, sacrifice, and human folly. Pietro paused under the cupola portraying the life of Moses. He looked around to see if anyone was close enough to hear his lowered voice.

"I had no luck with the names from Fumiani's ledger. Just as I expected all the Venetians were accounted for. Workmen from the mainland kept to themselves. They came and went. One day they were there, the next day they were gone, with no more loyalty than a Circassian mercenary. Their rent unpaid, they left behind meager goods not even worth the landlord's time to pawn with the Jews in the Ghetto. A few of the Venetian workmen remembered one or two of Fumiani's assistants but only by their nicknames. Fumiani was the one that was buried so they didn't worry themselves over men who weren't Venetians."

"So, they were no help?" Bigio asked.

"Not about the dead man."

Pietro put his hand on Bigio's arm and guided him even further away from the crowd to a corner across from the entrance. His voice became a whisper. "I don't want to muddy a clean man's cloak, but the world doesn't point a finger if you haven't done anything wrong."

Pietro stopped talking and waited while two priests walked by. "The workmen, especially the ones who worked longest on the church, complained to a man about the work starting and stopping. Zampelli said he was out of funds. Some weeks he couldn't even pay them in full for work they had done. More than once they got so fed up, they put down their tools until they were paid what was owed them. Zampelli was always crying poverty. All along the parishioners kept emptying their pockets and purses into his outstretched hands." Pietro bent close to Bigio. "The workmen wondered what spiritual needs required such constant attention at the convent of Saint Teresa."

The Serene Republic teemed with people ready to fill their pockets and roll down their stockings, but Bigio found it hard to believe that a voluptuary and thief hid under Zampelli's priestly robes. If Zampelli turned out to be a satyr and an embezzler, what did that have to do with the death of an itinerant worker and Fumiani fleeing his life?

Pietro obviously enjoyed the twists and turns of the winding path they were on. There was no surprise in the failings of a priest. He was after all human. While Pietro might relish Zampelli's hypocrisy, Bigio feared Pietro's suspicions would leave them floundering in the shoals of the lagoon far from solid ground. Why would Zampelli engage Bigio to find the truth if it would uncover his own misdeeds? It was hard to imagine a conscience so riven with guilt.

Bigio and Pietro walked out into San Marco crowded with pilgrims and tourists. They made their way to the arcade running the northern length of the square.

"Best for me to dig a little deeper into the life of our friend Zampelli. It's time for a haircut."

Pietro's hair was a stranger to scissors and comb. Bigio didn't remember it ever being other than a clump of matted straw. Pietro read Bigio's raised eyebrows and the quizzical tilt of his head.

"Now Master Bigio, you and my wife know I'm not that kind of man."

Young men and men who wanted to be thought young, their necks circled in gold chains, fingers bejeweled, and shirts open to display their perfumed chests, lounged in barber shops to make short-term acquaintances with men of their kind. If a man's interests ran to gossip and the latest political rumor and not an illicit rendezvous, a barbershop was also a fine place to spend time. Barbers knew the name, office, and ambition of everyone who sat in their chairs and passed by their windows on their daily rounds.

As scissors snapped and spies listened, sailors talked of their voyages and cargoes, soldiers complained about their senior officers, husbands groused about their wives, young rakes boasted of their conquests, and every Venetian had an opinion on the machinations in the Ducal Palace.

Pietro's hands flicked the hair edging over his ears. "A little off the side, I'll hear much better."

"Pietro, remember where we are. We're not on *terra firma* here. There's no bedrock, just rotten timbers and foul water."

"Don't worry, Master Bigio. I'm just a simple fruit monger."

That was what worried Bigio. He was poor, but he still was a patrician. If someone felt free to threaten him, what would stop them from destroying Pietro's stall or worse, harming his wife or daughter to send Bigio a message.

32

Bigio lay in bed staring at the ceiling, looking for angels and saints in the stains and cracked plaster. He found only hunchbacks, dwarves, and snarling wolves. He got up from bed, lit a candle, and began to leaf again through Fumiani's journals. They were his late-night companions, filling sleepless hours with angels and arches, alcove, balustrade, column, and cornice. Bigio imagined Fumiani, pen in hand, lips pursed, shading with delicate strokes courtyards and columned interiors of pure fantasy, then dissatisfied, turning the page, and beginning again. A lost man imagining ceilings he would never paint.

A moth circled above the open journal then flitted toward the candle. Bigio swung his hand to save the moth from the flame, hit the journal's edge, and it tumbled to the floor. When he picked it up, a folded sheet of paper fell on the floor next to the chair. The sheet was folded in quarters and smudged by dirty fingers that had opened and folded it many times. Scrawled in the corner on the back of the folded sheet in rough pencil, in what Bigio was sure was Fumiani's hand, were the words, "Mount Nebo." Bigio unfolded the paper, turned it over, and moved it under the circle of candlelight. An old woman, a shawl draped over her shoulders, held a taper in her hand. She bent over to light a candle in a row of candles. She wasn't a saint or a richly cloaked noble woman posing for the artist, just an ordinary old woman, wrinkled, concentrated in faith, lips parted in prayer. The artist came upon her standing before an altar in a side chapel and caught her with quick, fluid strokes in the act of praying. There was an immediacy to the drawing, an emotional connection between the artist and the woman. Even before Bigio saw the inscription on the bottom right of the sheet – "For Master Fumiani, Lucio da Nove" – he knew this was not the hand of Fumiani.

Bigio, clutching the journal, rose quickly from the chair and stumbled in his haste to pick up Fumiani's ledger resting on the chest at the foot of the bed. He turned to the last few pages and moved his finger down the list of names until he found the name he remembered. The faded ink sent a pulse through his finger. Bigio flipped through the pages of the journal and shook it upside down. No other sheets fell out. Fumiani took only this sheet when he fled and had kept it for four years. Bigio held the sheet in his hands. He looked at the old woman through the eyes of Fumiani, a lost man, a defeated man.

Zampelli motioned for Bigio to sit next to him on a bench in the sacristy. "Stefano, you have done a good job," Zampelli said. "I will write the priest in Nove to inquire about the man named Lucio. If he is the dead man, his family would be relieved though saddened to know what had happened."

"What did happen?" Bigio asked, his tone more impatient than he intended.

The priest's face reddened, "An accident, a workman fell from the scaffolding while putting on the finishing touches to the painting."

"Nothing more?"

"Accidents happen. I was wrong to think badly of poor Fumiani. He was under so much stress. The accident broke him, and he fled his life. That's what happened. Maybe he felt guilty for sending the man back up when the painting was finished. That's the worst I can say of him. We'll never know for certain. There are some mysteries

143

only God can solve. You've done all you can." Zampelli rose from the bench to signal their conversation was over.

"I'm a patient man." Bigio didn't get up. "I will wait till we hear from Nove."

A scowl flashed across Zampelli's face then quickly disappeared under his usual smile. "You're a good man, Stefano. That's why I asked you to help." He put his hand on Bigio's shoulder. "I trust you not to share what you've learned with anyone else until we are certain about this workman. You know I only have enough coffee money for one."

Bigio let his clumsy joke pass. Zampelli seemed anxious to make all the pieces of the puzzle fit and declare the investigation over. Bigio had never mentioned Pietro's name. He was certain Zampelli knew about him. "Mount Nebo. Father, does that mean anything to you?"

"Mount Nebo?" Zampelli paused for a moment to think. "That's where Moses is buried. It's where he looked out on the Promised Land that God forbade him to enter. Why do you ask?"

"Oh, it came up in café conversation." Zampelli didn't have to know everything.

33

Carla never took so much time at her toilette. Bigio waited in the parlor well beyond the time they planned to leave for San Sebastiano. When she finally appeared, she smelled of strong perfume. Her hair was combed into a chignon set with silver pins topped with pearls. She looked as if she were headed for a Carnival ball and not a small parish church. She wore a long, voluminous red silk dress and a light green silk cloak that Bigio had never seen before. It must have been stored away in her bedroom chest to be brought out for special occasions that would never come again. She wore long white gloves painted with faded red roses and clutched a handkerchief edged in gold thread – worn reminders of gay evenings long past.

Carla was unusually quiet despite her festive appearance. As the gondola passed under the bridge to Campo Carmini she grew more animated, her eyes enlivened by fond memories.

"Stefano, remember the Promenade in the Rio della Sensa? One year some fellow was so enamored of me he jumped off the bridge and swam toward the gondola and tried to clamber in. The gondolier had to push him away with his pole for fear he would upset the boat. Everyone on the bank and bridges was hooting and yelling."

"It wasn't me."

"Oh you foolish man. You knew you didn't have to do such wild things to have my affection."

The courtesans of the city had glided along the Rio della Sensa once a year in their luxurious, alluring finery. Two courtesans sat in the open felzes of most gondolas, but Carla always reigned alone. Men thronged the banks of the canal and the temporary wooden bridges. They hung over the balustrades and waved to get her attention. They whistled, pointed their fingers, and shouted coarse pleas for her company. She sat regally upright, staring straight ahead as if the adulation was her due. Workmen and citizens of moderate means dreamed of having the money to buy her companionship. Bigio watched, contented, knowing that she was his one day a week. The promenades stopped well over a dozen years ago. Carla had found excuses not to participate a decade or so earlier as younger courtesans now drew the stares, hurrahs, and dreams of soft breasts and embracing arms.

Their gondola glided up to the landing in front of San Sebastiano. The gondolier helped Carla and Bigio out of the boat. She tottered for a moment on her high platform clogs. Bigio placed his hand on her arm to steady her, a delicate porcelain doll calling with her fragile beauty for his protection.

Carla asked Bigio his previous Thursday to take her to see Veronese's ceiling in San Sebastiano. Veronese, buried in San Sebastiano, spent twenty years painting the interior of the church from the ceiling to the walls to the doors of the organ.

"Fumiani was a fine painter. His ceiling fills me with awe." Carla paused, searching for the right words. "Stefano, it is like like a young girl's reverence for a distant father. There is more warmth and light In Veronese, more feeling. Like a lover's embrace."

On Sunday Bigio took time to look up at Veronese's *Triumph of Venice* in the hall of the Great Council. He had paid little attention to it before. He imagined Fumiani standing beneath the painting in its carved and gilded oval frame, silently admiring the spiral columns, necklaced with clouds, that seemed to extend into the luminous blue sky beyond the ceiling itself.

Every surface of San Sebastiano shimmered and glowed with the satiny blues, reds, pinks, and greens that Bigio now recognized as Veronese's distinctive palette. Fumiani spoke with a solemn voice while Veronese sang. Carla stopped beneath the first of the three paintings framed in gilded wood that told the biblical story of Esther. She looked up, barely moving. Bigio heard her soft breathing in the empty church.

"Always the young beauties." Carla murmured to herself in a voice soft as a whisper.

Bigio followed Carla's eyes to the first painting. The pink cheeks, the flawless skin, the luminous blond curls. She could have been the young Carla that had so inflamed his heart. "Esther was lovely," Bigio said.

"Oh Stefano, that's not Esther, that's Vashti, the queen Ahasuerus spurned. He has banished her from the palace, she's walking down the stairs, not up."

Bigio looked again at the painting. His memory of the Old Testament tale was hazy, but now he understood why Carla had brought him here. What Carla wanted him to see, what connection she wanted him to make struck him full force. It was more than that Vashti's red dress and green cloak matched what Carla chose to wear that morning.

She took a few steps toward the second and larger rectangular painting and pointed her gloved hand toward it. "That's Esther. Most people come to see her coronation and the triumph of Mordecai in the next painting. I know Vashti has a haughty look about her, but she was the queen. Look how roughly she is being treated, Stefano. That guard is carrying the crown that once was hers. It saddens me to see her glance backward at the life she once lived, to the love she has lost."

Bigio turned around to look once more at Vashti's expulsion. Now he understood Veronese's intention: to better get the proper view, Bigio had to turn his back to the altar just as Vashti turned her back on Ahasuerus's order to attend a royal feast. The king, angry and insulted, turned his back on her. Now he understood the plea the painting was making for Carla.

"Promise me I won't be sent away to beg for my bread," Carla said.

"I've promised you."

Carla wanted the painting to speak for her, to make visible her fear of abandonment, the gnawing dread that, bereft of aging lovers, she would be reduced to penury. If it were anyone else, Bigio would have been offended that she doubted he would keep his word, that he would turn his back on her. Underneath his faded and frayed robes he remained a man of honor. Promises were to be kept, debts paid.

Carla placed her hand on his arm. "I know, but sometimes I worry." Bigio draped his arm over her shoulders and gently pulled her towards him. She rested her head on his shoulder. They stood in silence beneath the beautiful brush of Veronese.

Vashti descended and Esther ascended. Mordecai crowned with honor rose up on his white horse, while Haman bareheaded and dishonored tumbled into oblivion. If only justice was so clear-cut, if only heroes and villains so easily marked.

34

Pietro rubbed his hand slowly up and down a dark purple eggplant. A monger of nuts, beans, and dried fruit from the opposite stall wagged her finger at him and laughed.

"Master Stefano, look at the color of this fine specimen. Dark as a priest's cassock. You won't find one firmer than this fine fellow."

Bigio put his finger to his lips. Pietro picked up a peach and laid it next to the eggplant. "So sweet." He winked and lowered his voice. "From a nearby garden, but a costly pair from what I hear." He leaned close and whispered, "A bit of wine after a hard day's work? Campo San Trovaso after the Marangona."

The Marangona tolled as Bigio made his way toward the small corner café in the campo.

"Giovanni!" Bigio turned around at the greeting, as two young men embraced and walked off together. Bigio shook his head at his growing absorption in the life of a dead man.

Pietro was waiting, glass in his hand, broad smile on his face, a clear sign he knew something he was anxious to share with Bigio. Even before Bigio eased his body into the chair, Pietro began telling him what he had learned. "Beneath the smoke of workmen's chatter burned the fire of Zampelli's lust and pec…u…la…tion," a word Pietro spoke slowly, savoring the sounds of a word new to his vocabulary. "Our pious priest took himself regularly to the convent of Saint Teresa to hear confession and provide more than spiritual comfort to the flock in this supposed aviary of virgins. A few years before the new nave was roofed, a young nun at the convent couldn't hide the consequence of the carnal knowledge our learned priest had imparted to her. Too late to dispose of the child in her belly by forbidden measures common knowledge to experienced courtesans and prostitutes, Zampelli used church funds at his disposal to make sure the infant boy went quickly from convent to the home of the priest's barren sister in Piovega."

Pietro took a sip of wine and paused for dramatic effect, like an actor before his final oration to a hushed audience. "Money that should have gone to rebuilding the church went to the convent to keep things quiet and to the priest's sister who raised the boy alone after her husband, an honest but poor mason, died a few months after the child was taken in."

Pietro leaned back in his chair, proud of what his sleuthing had uncovered. "I am not a man to besmirch another man's reputation, especially a priest's. This was no idle rumor. Like a sailor plotting his position from several landmarks along the shore, I talked to a handful of people till the lines intersected. This Zampelli is more man than priest, master Bigio."

Bigio had lived too long in Venice to be shocked or even surprised by Zampelli's weakness and lies, by the wide gap between words and deeds, between reputation and reality. In Venice men were made of flesh and blood, while saints were fashioned from paint and marble. Bigio once saw a masked nobleman on all fours scrounging for fallen coins under the gaming tables at the Ridotto. He saw men with noble names and revered ancestors sell their principles in the Broglio. He witnessed bribes offered and sought. He watched noblemen brought low by misfortune and driven by greed shed their dignity and let their stoles hang from their arms to signal their willingness to exchange their votes for money and favors. Nominations were bartered like cheap goods on the Rialto. Men he once admired cast aside honor and the decrees of the Republic to go from bench to bench in the Great Council asking for votes and threatening those of firmer virtue who were committed to following their conscience. Round after round of blind drawings and elaborate electoral procedures for doge and other high offices were convoluted exercises in pessimism, a clear-eyed admission of man's base and corrupt nature. In Venice, vices strutted about in bright sunlight, while the seven virtues hung in the shadows on church walls.

Every other patrician family seemed to have a daughter exiled to a nunnery, some for safekeeping until marital alliances could be negotiated, others, with older, more beautiful sisters, forever. Some exiled nuns gave their souls to Christ, others their bodies to pleasure. There was no need to talk to the nun. If Zampelli seduced her, she was shamed enough. Seduced or seducer, it was clear Zampelli was a hypocrite and possibly worse a thief who robbed his own flock.

From what Pietro heard, it didn't appear that Zampelli was still siphoning funds from donations raised for rebuilding the church. For the last year or so workmen were paid regularly. The priest's bastard was now a young man, a mason like the man he thought was his father, supporting his mother as a good son should.

"Did Fumiani know of the embezzlement?"

Pietro shook his head. "One mystery at a time. That I don't know...yet."

Did Zampelli's son really matter, or was it only a spicy tale for workmen and parishioners of San Pantalon to savor? It only mattered if Fumiani knew or someone thought he knew. If either one was the case.... Bigio didn't want to follow the logic for it would lead to graver failings than lust. Did Zampelli have Lucio da Nove killed to frighten Fumiani into silence and four years later riven by guilt ask someone to uncover his crime? Guilt had a rapacious appetite. It could gnaw a man's soul to the core, but this made no sense.

Bigio counted out the coins for the wine and put it next to

Pietro's empty glass. He stared at the coins and circled them with his fingers for a moment or two. Dozens of workmen worked for decades to build San Pantalon. Dozens of workmen wondered why they had to wait so long to be paid for their labor. Zampelli's bastard must have lived very well.

35

Zampelli gulped air to compose himself. Tears trickled down his flushed cheeks. He admitted his own failing. He was certain Fumiani didn't know or even suspect his illegitimate child and the money he siphoned for his care. Bigio wanted the priest to be shaken, to tremble with remorse at his lies and thievery, but his tears made Bigio uncomfortable. A man could cry over the pain of others but not when the pain was of his own making, pain caused by disloyalty to himself.

"Didn't Fumiani complain about the slowness of the rebuilding?"

"A grumble or two perhaps. But Giovanni was a perfectionist. So was Comino. If anything slowed things down, it was their wanting everything to be just right. Giovanni was a man not satisfied with mediocrity. That's why I wanted him to paint the ceiling."

Though no one else was in the church, Zampelli looked toward the entrance to make sure they were alone and lowered his voice, "Stefano, I admit I took what wasn't mine. It was a sin. But I didn't do it for myself. I live a simple life. I did it so the child wouldn't suffer, wouldn't live his life without a family to love him. I took just enough to keep my sister and the child from starving. Don't believe all you hear. Workmen exaggerate. They always think others live better than they do. My sister is a frugal woman. Pardon me Stefano, but the child didn't live like a patrician."

What patricians was he talking about? He hoped the child lived better than he had these last thirty years, but Bigio didn't say anything – he didn't want the priest's pity.

"What else haven't you told me?"

"Nothing," Zampelli tugged on his wattle.

Bigio wanted to believe the priest had stopped lying. He wanted to believe he was telling the truth until he saw again the tug, the tic of a troubled soul. Later, when Bigio walked through their conversation again, he cursed himself for a mistake only a novice would make. He let his anger at Zampelli for lying get in the way of finding out the truth. He asked if it was true that the priest stole from the church to pay for the upbringing of his illegitimate child. Zampelli seemed too ready – almost relieved – to admit his failing of the flesh.

36

The city grew smaller as the boat headed out into open water. The waves slapped roughly against the sides of the boat. He was surrounded by grim strangers who didn't answer when Bigio asked where they were going. The sky darkened, and the sea turned more turbulent. The waves thumped against the bow loud and insistent.

The pounding on the door became louder. "Master Bigio," a high-pitched voice called his name. "Master Bigio!"

"Who is it?" Bigio's voice dry and rough with sleep.

"Pietro sent me."

Bigio sat up slowly and dangled his feet over the edge of the bed to get the blood flowing. If he stepped too quickly onto the floor, the soles of his feet felt as if they were pierced by hundreds of needles. He shuffled across the room and cracked open the door. A young boy, no more than ten or eleven, whom Bigio had never seen before, stood at the door, roughly dressed, and by sight and smell in need of soap and water.

"Pietro says come quickly to San Pantalon." He turned and scuttled toward the stairs.

"What time is it?" Bigio asked, still muzzy with sleep.

The boy disappeared down the stairs. Bigio opened the shutters to a slate gray sky and an empty Campo San Barnaba. Pietro should have been busy setting up his stall. What could be so important that it couldn't wait till midday, so immediate that he would sacrifice a handful of morning lira? Bigio dressed as quickly as his aching body allowed.

Bigio walked across the bridge to San Margherita. The market was just beginning to rouse its from slumber. Pietro's stall was shrouded in canvas. Bigio paused to catch his breath at the top of the bridge leading to San Pantalon. He saw a half-dozen workers from the market clustered at the stepped landing in front of the church. He looked for Pietro's white-haired mop. Bigio didn't see him.

Bigio approached the landing. He was about to wave good morning to the mongers. But then he saw their grim expressions and lowered his hand. At the sight of his black patrician's robe, they spread out to let him through.

Four steps of the landing were above water, the fifth and last step was partially submerged. A few melons floated out toward the middle of the canal. Bigio first saw white tendrils entwined with the green moss that clung to the steps. It was Pietro's hair. His body had been wedged in the bottom step. Someone didn't want it to float away. Melons and apples bulged beneath the fruit monger's soaked white tunic. Wisps of blood floated around the body. If he had been killed at the steps, there would have been more blood. Pietro must have been killed elsewhere and his body brought to San Pantalon. His corpse brought here to send a message, to teach others a lesson – that was what the workers from the market thought. Pietro skirted the regulations one too many times, one of them said, pointing to Pietro's shirt stuffed with the fruits of his illicit labor. Right, another fellow said, he didn't play by the rules and get in line for his goods like the rest of us.

Every man, even the lowliest laborer, thought he stood at the center of the world. Did a market monger really think the Council of Ten would kill one of them over a basket of plums? There was a message in Pietro's poor body stuck in the slimy steps of the canal. Bigio knew it wasn't intended for the fruit and vegetable mongers of the Serene Republic. Otherwise why send the boy to fetch him. The coward who killed Pietro didn't want Bigio to hear about it secondhand. He wanted Bigio to see the defiled body floating in front of the church.

Bigio gripped the lion's head handle of his cane. His hand shook with an anger that seized his entire body. He stepped back as two workers walked down the landing steps and lifted up Pietro's body. Rotting melons fell to the ground and rolled back into the canal.

Bigio had accepted Zampelli's offer to find out the truth of Fumiani's "death" and disappearance because the priest had been of service to his family. He accepted because he couldn't abide that a dead man was buried without name and prayer, while in some distant town a wife and mother wondered what had become of the man they loved. A lost bird was an affront, a friend murdered a deep and personal wound. He lived too long in a city where everything had a price, where the powerful bought and sold principles as easily as a handful of cockles, to believe Justice would triumph. Neither she nor Bigio were blind. Like Pietro said, someone should pay. He would make sure of it.

Bigio stood mute with anger and guilt, looking down at the pale body lying on the campo stones. Bigio heard a jagged scream. He turned to see Pietro's wife rushing down the steps of the bridge. Maria hurried behind clutching her mother's worn cloak. Pietro's wife's outstretched hands grasped the empty air, as she ran wailing toward the body. Bigio had no words for the innocent victims of his honor. He turned away and headed home, swinging his cane in a wide, violent arc.

37

Bigio spent the next two days in his room, exhausted by anger. Anger at those who had killed Pietro. Anger at himself for drawing Pietro into an affair that had nothing to do with him. Pietro owed Zampelli nothing. He wasn't haunted by the dead workman. He was drawn by the mystery and by his desire to help a lame friend whom he thought needed his aid. Now he was dead because of Bigio.

There was a heavy knock on the door. No one came to Bigio's apartment in the evening. The boy bringing his polenta came early in the morning. The arthritic patrician across the hall came in the afternoon to talk of the past and complain about the present and never left his own rooms once the sun went down. Carla never sent her maid at night with good news or bad. Better an assassin with a knife or knotted garrote than the maid with grim news of her mistress.

"Master Bigio, are you there." A deep voice he heard before but couldn't place.

Nicolas Taliaferro stood at the door, face grim and flushed, not, Bigio was certain, from walking up three flights. He walked in without a word and sat at the table. Bigio put a small plate of grapes in front of him. Nicolas pushed the plate away.

"You should have told me. You lied."

"I didn't lie, I just didn't tell you the truth. It wasn't the time. When did you find out?"

"Yesterday afternoon. After your friend's death. If you want to know the secrets of Venice, come to an apothecary."

"What else does everyone know?"

"Only that Giovanni died twice. That's all." Nicolas stared at Bigio. "When I heard, I was boiling. I wanted to come here and spit in your face. Yelled so much, brought my wife to tears. Why do you want to spit at that poor patrician? she said. You should spit on Giovanni's grave – he was the one who made a widow of Laura before her time, though God knows she was no saint. When you came to see my uncle, I didn't tell the truth either. I wanted to protect my uncle and the memory of my cousin. A man should protect his family, even those in heaven."

Bigio let him speak the truth without interruption. Giovanni loved Laura. She was a supplicant before Saint Roch, a luminous angel floating among the clouds and the Virgin herself. She was in everything he painted. But they grew apart. She wanted the good life. He wanted heaven. She was right to worry about her health after their first child was stillborn and the second lost in the womb, but Laura was, Nicolas admitted, a vain woman who cared more for her figure than a family. Giovanni wanted sons he could pass his skills onto, a family to stand beside the Bellinis and Tintorettos. She wasn't a bad wife. She doted on him like young wives do with an older husband. She worried he would grow old and infirm before he received the rewards his talents deserved, the rewards she passionately wanted for herself. They ate well. She had a cassone and cabinet full of fine clothes of the latest fashion. Giovanni had his art. He didn't need liveried servants, gilded mirrors, Belgian tapestries, and silver candelabras to be happy. The only time Nicolas heard his cousin blaspheme was when talk of money came up. Her face darkened, and her beauty disappeared behind a dark scowl. She cursed painters in shoddy shops with backrooms of foreign lackeys who pumped out works at the lowest price. They stole bread from the table of true artists and would drive them all to penury. She barely listened when Fumiani calmly argued that these second-rate daubers were not his rivals for commissions and patrons. What more can I do, he asked Nicolas. He wouldn't waste his time doing portraits, painting small pieces for private altars, or cranking out cheap devotional paintings for wealthy Englishmen. When a laborer wasn't working, he was drinking. When Fumiani wasn't painting, he was drawing. When he wasn't drawing, he was thinking about drawing. You cannot create the vastness of heaven on the cheap and quick he told Laura. Patience he told her, patience.

Nicolas paused and shook his head. "She ran out of patience. Sometimes, I think my cousin was too beautiful for her soul's good. She believed life would reward her for her beauty. She was more disappointed when it didn't than a plain woman who grew up expecting less from life. To keep her happy, to give her another silk dress or two, Giovanni did something he told me he would never do – he copied a painting. I never saw him so sad and beaten down when he came to the shop to tell me what he had done. The monks of San Nicolas Maggiore ate their humble bread and soup beneath Veronese's wedding scene at Cana in silent awe of Christ's miracle, while Fumiani's copy, shrunk by a third, hung in a palazzo on the Brenta to impress and amuse a patrician's guests stuffing their bellies with fine wine and rich food. Never again, Giovanni said, never again."

"He painted for Ferdinando de'Medici," Bigio said. "A rich patron, just what his wife would have wanted."

"The Prince came too late. She had grown bitter. It was the ceiling. It took over his life." He clasped his hands under his chin and looked down at the table. He hesitated for a moment before looking up. "After my cousin died, my wife and I went through her belongings to see what we would keep and what we should give to the poor. My wife found in the bottom of the marriage cassone under two dresses she didn't remember Laura wearing more than once, if at all. These dresses were carefully folded. Underneath them we found her betrothal portrait. The drawing was foxed at the edges, crunched in one corner, and creased across her cheek. How could she have treated so carelessly a drawing done with such love?"

"Why are you telling me all this?" Bigio asked.

"If you are looking for the truth, you must hear the truth. It seemed like part of the puzzle, though I'm not sure how it all fits." Nicolas looked pale and exhausted from his revelations, long suppressed by love and loyalty.

This happened, then that happened: you could chart the sequence of acts, their causes and consequences. That was the easiest part to detail and decipher in any investigation. The human heart with its chambers of desire and regret, that was the deepest mystery.

Bigio apologized to Nicolas for his silence at the apothecary. The real reason for his apology went unspoken. He made a decent man say more than he wanted, made him bear the pain of buried truths.

38

Bigio had no feathered companion to listen to his complaints, no smiling friend to hand him a plum or a handful of grapes to start his day. If God wanted him injured but not dead, he was doing a damn good job of it. He stood at the back of San Pantalon during Pietro's funeral mass. He avoided Zampelli and spoke only a few hollow words of comfort to Pietro's sobbing widow. He read the blame in her eyes. He left the church quickly in need of fresh air.

His aimless wandering took him to I Frari. He hadn't in the past been moved by Titian's *Assumption of the Virgin*, praised by all. Mary floated on a layer of clouds while God and her crown awaited, and an awe-struck crowd gestured and pointed from below. He thought the painting simple and schematic. This morning Mary's red gown glowed in the golden light of heaven as she raised her arms to greet her heavenly Father. What before he saw as a theatrical pose now struck him as a woman trembling with anxious anticipation, like a child about to be reunited with her father returning from the war or a long voyage.

While he stood looking up at the painting with fresh eyes, a man and woman whom he took to be husband and wife placed vases of flowers on either side of the altar. She fussed over the arrangement. She looked at one of the vases, moved it a few inches to the right, gently rearranged a few of the blooms, stepped back to look at the vase, and then moved it again half as much in the opposite direction. She stepped back once more, looked at her handiwork, and nodded in approval, satisfied that the flowers and the position of the jars were where they should and could only be.

What if Fumiani climbed up and down the scaffolding to look at the color and shading of a column, what if he spent several days retouching the folds of a cloak or the tensed muscles of a naked back until it was perfect in his eyes? Bigio felt a kinship to this man he never met. He was a man who didn't throw away his honor for a handful of coins. Who was Cassana with his viper's tongue to mock him for his diligence, to claim that the ceiling was full of figures but not life? In a small place like Venice, Fumiani likely heard the whispered insults. The patricians, who, seeing the ceiling with the Electress, praised the painting for its size, were Philistines who gave him no solace. Was he nothing more than a Carnival dancing dog applauded for staying up on his hind legs for a minute or two? Fumiani believed he was blessed with gifts from God. Not to exercise them to the fullest, no matter how long it took, was more than a waste of canvas and paint. It was an affront to God himself.

39

"May I join you?" A short man masked in a white bauta sat down in the chair opposite Bigio without waiting for his answer.

"Do I have a choice?"

"Of course, we are creatures of God and have free will. But in this case, no. Please do drink your coffee before it turns cold."

The only customers in the café were Bigio and two old men hunched over in conspiratorial conversation in a corner table. Savoring his afternoon coffee, Bigio hadn't seen the man enter, followed by a stocky man in a black mask who now sat by the door watching them both. Bigio recognized the man in the black mask as the fellow who had been shadowing him. The man sitting opposite Bigio wore a tri-cornered hat, a wide black cape that reached almost to his knees, and a black mantle that covered his shoulders. His white half mask covered his face to just below the nose. He was a patrician who didn't want to be recognized. He waved to the café boy to bring him a cup of coffee and a plate of *zaletti*. What struck Bigio besides the man's affected, theatrical manner of speaking were his crimson leather gloves tight as a second skin and his highly polished black leather boots.

"Choice, an appropriate word for my purpose, I would say," the man said.

From his voice and carriage Bigio guessed he was in his late twenties at most. His manner reminded him of the pompous Pantaleone, full of self-importance and unsolicited advice. Give him a brown mask with a hooked nose, a double pointed beard, a pair of red tights, and a small knife hanging from his bag, and this young fop would be ready for the commedia dell'arte. Bigio was sure that his silent companion sitting by the door had a very sharp knife and no sense of humor.

"Choice, yes choice. God's gift of redemption to fallen man, wouldn't you say, Master Bigio?"

"And you are?"

"A friend, Master Bigio, a friend."

"My friends have names."

The fellow paid no attention. "It's over. Leave it alone. He's long dead. She's dead. It does no one any good to rattle their bones."

She? Bigio tried not to show his confusion. The man obviously thought Bigio knew more than he did. Bigio wanted him to keep talking, hoping he would tell him what he didn't know.

"I am told you are a smart man. Be smart, let it lie. Don't go rooting around like a wild boar."

"I just want to find out the truth."

"How quaint. You want the truth? I will tell you the one big truth. The less you know, the better for you. The more you know, the worse for you."

"Like Pietro?"

The man shook his head with a studied expression of remorse that couldn't disguise his disdain. "Some overly enthusiastic fellows, they got carried away. A good beating would have been enough. Accidents happen." He picked up a *zaletto* delicately between thumb and forefinger and dipped it into his coffee. "We have many fruit mongers in Venice. One less is no loss to the Republic." He chewed the cookie slowly. He wiped the crumbs from his lips. "Master Bigio, have you ever seen the slaughter of the pigs in the Piazetta in the last days of Carnival?" He went on, not caring if Bigio answered yes or no. "Quite the sport. The creatures are set free and go scuttling and slipping and squealing over the stones with no place to hide. Butchers' apprentices chase them to the shouts and laughter of the crowd. They round them all up and hand them over to their masters in the guild who butcher the pigs on the spot and distribute the meat to the crowd. The doge himself and officers of the Republic watch with pleasure from the balcony above. They do enjoy the spectacle. The spilling of blood does not bother them at all. It is part of their duty. They do it to keep the citizens happy. To keep the Republic serene." He took a last, long sip of coffee. He removed several coins from a leather pouch and placed them on the table. "I am sorry to have interrupted your pleasure. I know how much you enjoy a good cup of coffee. Please have another. I insist." The man rose, bowed slightly and turned to leave.

"What about Fumiani?"

"The painter, what about him? He's no concern of mine. I heard it was an accident." He smiled, "Accidents happen."

The man walked toward the door.

"This won't end because you want it to. Pietro was a friend."

His silent companion opened the door. The young patrician left without turning around. He had said what he wanted to say. What Bigio said or felt was of no concern to him. Did he speak for himself or was he a messenger boy for those who didn't dirty their hands with threats or hide in dark alleys with drawn knives. Bigio would find out who this pompous fellow with the crimson gloves and polished boots was. He would find out whom he was protecting, whose bones he didn't want disturbed, whose names he didn't want sullied. No one killed a fruit monger and threatened a patrician, even a poor old one, to protect the good name of a butcher or a bricklayer.

40

Bigio slept fitfully. He barely touched his morning polenta. He should never have involved Pietro. A week had passed, and Pietro's death was a canker on his soul. He had never forsaken his Thursday with Carla, but he knew he would be dark company. He wrote a note saying he wouldn't be visiting this week and blamed his indisposition on the weather. Perhaps it was bile from the anger and remorse bubbling inside of him, or maybe the words he wrote gave his body permission to abandon its defenses. He took ill and spent two fevered days in bed able only to sip broth and eat a bit of stale bread.

He hoped to look for the man with the crimson gloves at the Sunday meeting of the Great Council but felt too weak to make the trip across the Grand Canal. Instead he sat in bed with Fumiani's drawings spread out over his worn coverlet. Bigio clung to the hope of finding clues hidden among the angels and angles, a message encoded in the cornices, columns, and capitals. Fumiani taught him to pay more attention to what before had been the decorative and unnoticed background to his dull, repetitive life. If there were clues in the drawings, they eluded him. What he did see was a man obsessed: constantly reaching for the right line, the right shading and shadow, the right slant of an angel's head, the perfect smile, the perfect aureole of ringlets. Bigio had never been possessed by such a passion. He had lived a stunted life of accepted pleasures. He had never been consumed by anything, not even regret.

Late Monday morning, Carla's maid, who rarely came to his room, brought a warm rice torte and a note from her mistress wishing him a speedy return to good health and asking him to come to her home late Wednesday afternoon. Carla didn't explain why she wanted him to come on Wednesday, the Admiral's day. He assumed he was to come in the afternoon because her other remaining patron would arrive in the early evening for the pleasure of her company. Or perhaps the old man's gout had flared up, and she wanted to make up for the day he missed.

In the mid-afternoon Zampelli sent over a young boy with a note confirming what Bigio already knew, that the man buried in the church was Lucio da Nove. Now his wife would be a respected village widow and not an object of whispers and innuendo about a wayward husband who left her for another woman. Now his young son could remember his father as a good man who went away to support his family and not a wastrel who deserted them. Now memories would be cherished and burnished. One debt was now paid to the dead but not in full. Not yet.

41

Bigio heard the deep rumble of a man's laughter when he entered the foyer. He told Carla's maid he would return when her mistress wasn't engaged. She said her mistress had ordered her to bring him upstairs when he arrived. He had shared Carla for almost forty years and knew some of her companions by name and others as nodding acquaintances in the Great Council, but he had never shared the parlor with any of them. It wasn't done. A courtesan's company was enjoyed in private.

"Stefano, I am sure you know Admiral Moroni."

Bigio recognized from Carla's sly smile that he and the Admiral being there together was no accident. Bigio bowed slightly, "By his glorious reputation only." The Admiral rose and extended his hand. He had a strong handshake for a man of his years. He wore a well-powdered wig. A thin scar slashed across his right cheek – from some battle or duel of honor Bigio imagined.

"Carla tells me of your recent ill health. I pray you are feeling better."

Bigio thanked him for his concern while trying to disguise his irritation with Carla for sharing the failings of his body with another.

"The death of one's friend can be a great blow." The Admiral paused, bit his lower lip, and nodded his head up and down in sad recollection. "At the siege of Negroponte, I lost my aide to the plague. We had come through many battles together. He was like a son to me. I couldn't eat for days and barely slept. I've seen many men die, some in my arms. But his death…his death pierced my heart like a rapier's thrust. But we must go on. It is our duty."

Bigio glanced at Carla and then the Admiral, ready to pretend that he didn't understand what he was talking about.

"Stefano, Venice is a great power but a small city. News of ill fortune travels quickly. The death of your friend is the talk from San Marco to the Rialto. Carla thought I might be of some assistance."

The Admiral's offer of help would come to nothing. The Admiral probably had nothing better to do and was looking to fill his empty hours. Bigio doubted he could be of any help, a man of almost eighty who had not served the Republic since the Venetian defeat at Chios over fifteen years before, whose fingers were no longer on the pulse of power. Whatever rumors he might hear would be stale murmurs from the Rialto.

Bigio was moved by Carla's concern. He didn't want to insult the Admiral who likely saw his assistance as one last campaign in a glorious but now quiescent life. He didn't want the Admiral asking questions under the Ducal portico. He didn't need another innocent man roiling the waters. One dead friend was enough.

"My dear Admiral, thank you for your offer. I will tell you what I know. But it mustn't go any further than this parlor. I welcome your advice, but I alone have to find out the truth about Fumiani. And why Pietro was killed."

"Not who killed him?" the Admiral asked.

"Why will be easier."

"How can there be justice if those *who*," the Admiral pronounced the word as if it were in capital letters, "aren't punished for their crimes."

"Admiral, you have seen more of Venetian justice than I. You must know that in Venice the law and justice often go their separate ways. Best leave punishment to God. I'm sure Carla has told you that Father Zampelli asked me to unravel the mystery of Fumiani's death. I said yes because the priest was a friend to my father and brother. I said yes because it offended me that a man died name-less. Now I do it for Pietro Acconci. He was a man impossible to dislike. There are few men I can say that about. He died because he was trying to help me. Call it punishment or whatever you like, someone must pay."

"That sounds like justice to me." The Admiral turned to Carla, "Please have your maid bring us some glasses so we can enjoy the wine I brought. And now, Stefano, tell me about this Fumiani affair. Of course I know of Fumiani and his marvelous painting, but I never met the man nor have I seen the ceiling. I take mass and light candles at my parish church, San Stefano."

The Admiral sat silently rubbing his thumb back and forth across his lips and running a finger up and down his scar as he listened to Bigio detail what he knew and didn't know. Bigio ended his monologue by describing the masked patrician's veiled threats at the café.

"Of course, this coward who threatened you didn't tell you his name. Do you remember ever seeing him at the Great Council?"

All Bigio knew was that he was a bit of a fop with his theatrical manner, his crimson gloves, and boots polished bright as a mirror. The Admiral nodded, "One fop among many. We live in decadent age, Stefano. The young men of the Republic spend more time at their toilette than their sisters. I may have seen this fellow, but there are so many like him. And this priest Zampelli, I have heard talk of him. I think he's a friend of the Querinis."

"He did mention that he travelled to Ravello with a cousin of the dogaressa."

The Admiral grimaced at the mention of her name. "I have always been a loyal citizen and a patriot, but she tested my loyalty when she was alive, and now that she is dead I have nothing good to say about her and the cipher that was her husband. They dined and danced while good men died under Turkish sword and shot. They were blind to the sacrifice of others or simply didn't care. Banquets and balls, they carried on as if the Republic's coffers were full, as if the war with the Turks cost us nothing. What profligates. They lived in extravagance until the very end."

"Was it all her doing? What about Silvestro?"

"He was not cut from the same cloth as his father. She wanted him to be doge more than he. I think he would have been happy to live well in his own palazzo, but she wanted to live in the Palace." The Admiral looked at Carla. "I don't mean any offense to your charms. But he was a weak man in her thrall. She had certain courtesan arts to say it as delicately as I can."

Carla sighed, "I thought her a good woman."

"Oh, she was charitable. I can't argue that. She flung money from the balcony of the Palace and gave bread and wine to the poor. Where did that money come from? From whose pocket? My dear, what is more important, how one gains one's money or how one spends it? Grapes from bad soil do not produce good wine."

The Admiral took a sip of wine, put down his glass and cast his eyes toward the floor, speaking as if he were asking Bigio's forgiveness. "I regret my vote for Silvestro. It was an honest vote. I asked for nothing and took nothing, unlike many of our fellows. I thought him a harmless man who would do no mischief. I didn't think hard enough about the profligacy of his wife."

Bigio had heard the gossip swirling around Silvestro Valiero's election but paid no attention to it. Electoral bribery and favors traded in the Broglio were nothing new. Only children and the English charmed by appearances and proclamations believed that in Venice the office sought the man. The law that forbade patricians from shaking hands or embracing after an election in the Great Council carried no more weight than a hummingbird's wing. Everyone knew the Republic had the best office holders that money and favors could buy. All that changed were the players and the ingeniousness of their deceit, whether it was a counterfeit gold ball drawn from the urn or a gang of conspirators working together to fiddle with the ballots without being seen. Their machinations didn't matter to Bigio. Doges came and went, and he remained poor and lame.

"I will leave the defense of the Valieros and the Querinis to their toadies. What baffles me is what their ambition has to do with a poor parish priest?

"A poor parish priest who has lied to you more than once. Who, for whatever altruistic excuse he hides behind, has stolen from his own church."

"Yes, Zampelli has lied to me and stolen money from his church, whether for his sister and child or to help Elisabetta and Silvestro buy their way into the Ducal Palace. But I have known him too long to believe he was involved in the murder of Pietro. He's too weak a man for such treachery. But what if some suspicious fool among the Querinis thought my digging around in the past would harm the family's future pursuit of power and killed a nosey fruit monger to make him drop his investigation? I wouldn't want to get you caught up in his suspicions."

"Stefano, I appreciate your concern over my well-being, but don't worry about my safety. My service to the Republic and gray hairs will protect me from any hot heads. It will be better for you if we are seen together. We will go on Sunday to find the man in the crimson gloves. I will be the shield your friend Pietro couldn't be."

The Admiral grew quiet for a moment, lost in past campaigns and victories. "I'm a man of faith and admire our martyrs for their constancy, but you don't win battles with dead men. I'm not sure which is worse, reckless courage or timidity. I will never forgive Mocenigo for his spiritless abandonment of the siege in '92. If we had taken Crete, we would have avoided seven more years of war and the death of many men. Not to mention the draining of the Treasury. We will proceed with firmness and purpose. Remember, preparation and strategy, Stefano, preparation and strategy."

42

Over a thousand of Bigio's fellow patricians walked into the Hall of the Great Council in solemn scarlet procession, their eyes looking downward or straight ahead. They sat listening to an official drone on about the shocking licentious freedom of nobles who flaunted edicts about proper dress and behavior. They didn't seem to notice or had stopped looking at the paintings that surrounded them, the victories on the walls, the heavenly glory in ornate gilded frames above them. Veronese's Venice sat in her rich silk gown above them on a throne of clouds. Tintoretto's *Paradise*, crowded as San Marco during the Festa della Sensa, stretched across the wall at the far end of the hall. The masterpieces of the Republic's most honored artists were mere backdrop to the prattling of men whose names no one would remember in two generations.

Arms crossed to hide the frayed sleeves of his moth-eaten scarlet robe, Bigio looked from the painted heavens above to the pale faces of the patricians sitting on the nearby benches. He and the Admiral didn't see the fop with the crimson gloves when they made their way across the crowded courtyard of the Ducal Palace and up the stairs leading to the Great Council. The Admiral did all he could to draw attention to their apparent friendship. He walked next to Bigio, whispered conspiratorially in his ear, smiled, laughed, and patted him fraternally on the shoulder. As they walked through the courtyard clustered with patricians and commoners, patricians doffed their hats and put their right hands on their hearts in traditional greeting. Some of the older commoners, who remembered the Admiral's service during the Turkish war, bowed and a few old comrades lightly applauded as he passed by.

When the deliberations were over, Bigio walked out of the Great Hall, close by the Admiral's side. They stopped in the arcade just outside the Palace's main gates where small groups of patricians clustered. "Crowded as a morning market. Here our corrupt fellows bring their fresh votes to sell," the Admiral whispered.

The Admiral tugged lightly on Bigio's sleeve and motioned with a quick flick of his head to the right where a group of ten or so patricians were huddling. Those in their late twenties gestured in youthful animation, while old men with lined faces bent over their canes to catch the words of their more subdued middle-aged kin.

"The Querinis," the Admiral said.

The Querini family claimed with boastful pride their descent from the Roman nobles who settled in the lagoon at the very beginning of Venetian history. The Admiral rattled off offices that the Querinis held past and present: Council against Blasphemy, Council of Ten, Great and Little Sages, chief judicial magistrates, Lords of the Night.

"There's more," he said. "Major to minor, they are everywhere. A future doge stands among them if they have their way. Their business is power…"

"And my poking around is bad for business."

Venice was dying, and the Querinis wanted to be the crown on the corpse. What vain ambition, what fleeting glory, thought Bigio. To paint heaven and the glory of a martyred saint was a more worthy ambition.

The Querinis fluttered about the Piazza San Marco like a flock of cardinals ready to take flight. One among them turned around, and Bigio saw his crimson-gloved hand slash the air to make a point. He couldn't see if his boots were polished shiny as black marble, but he was certain from his body and carriage that he was the young man from the café. Bigio struck the tip of his cane sharply on the Piazza stones to get the Admiral's attention.

The Admiral saw the man and slowly walked over to the eldest among the Querinis. He took his hat off with an operatic flourish of his left hand, put his right hand on his heart, and bent low to kiss with florid deference the edge of the elderly man's trembling sleeve. He asked after his health and the health of his family. The Admiral paused, "Pardon my impoliteness. Let me introduce my dear friend, Stefano Bigio. I am sure you remember his brother Gregorio, so unfortunately lost at sea many years ago."

The old man, his eyes red-rimmed and cloudy, hoarsely greeted Bigio and extended his arm for a palsied handshake. Bigio caught the eye of the man with the crimson gloves. The man stared straight past him with a frozen smile thin as a scar. The Admiral guided the elder Querini off to the side to speak to him alone. Bigio strained to hear what they were saying. They spoke for a few minutes, their conversation muffled by the sounds of the Piazza. They walked slowly back to Bigio and the rest of the Querinis. The Admiral apologized for not staying, but they had to be on their way. He wished the old man continued good health. After a few steps, Bigio and the Admiral were swallowed up by the late afternoon crowd filling the Piazza.

"Old Antonio is past the age of ambition. He will soon meet Saint Peter. His nephew Flavio did not act on his instruction. For what reason, Antonio does not know or claims not to know. A fruit monger means nothing to him. And no offense, Stefano, but you are the last of the Bigios and no consequence to him." The Admiral touched Bigio's sleeve as if to soften the harsh truth of the old man's words. "They will take care of the ruffians who killed your friend."

"The thugs who killed Pietro and dumped his body in the canal were just following orders. They did what they were paid to do. Flavio is the one with blood on his hands. He has to pay."

"I will witness your good name, Stefano."

Bigio didn't answer. Venice was a nest of vipers, brothers denouncing brothers who cheated them out of their inheritance, jealous wives denouncing their husbands for blasphemy in revenge for their adultery, merchants denouncing their rivals for adulterating oil or cheating on their taxes. Bigio never fed the *bocca di leone*, but if he stayed silent, then he was no better than one of the thugs helping to wedge Pietro's body on the landing stairs. He would write the truth, and the Admiral would attest to his honorable intentions. A man was never too old to be loyal to his friends and loyal to himself.

He had enough of Zampelli's lies. It was time to find out if he was more than just friends with the Querinis. "I will talk to Zampelli."

"If my presence will be helpful, I will go with you to talk to this priest."

"Thank you, but this is something I have to do myself."

"Preparation and strategy, Stefano, preparation and strategy."

43

The visit to San Sebastiano had been a rare excursion outside her parlor for Carla and Bigio. He worried about her frailness amidst the crowds of foreigners who clogged the narrow streets never quite sure where they were and young apprentices who rushed carelessly on their errands afraid their masters would take a hand to them if they were late. A second outing a few weeks later, this time to San Zanipolo, was also Carla's idea. Carla knew the twists and turns and blind alleys of his investigation. Silvestro Valiero and his father were buried in the church along with other doges from past centuries. Maybe the dead, she said, would speak to Bigio more clearly than the living. Before Fumiani's second death, Bigio thought such talk the hollow pieties of priests and old women who believed in spirits and the oracular power of tarot cards. Fumiani taught him that the dead can speak through pen and brush though their voices may be faint, and the meaning of their words mixed and muffled. Bigio wasn't sure a sculptor paid to glorify the dead could speak truthfully with chisel and marble. He would humor Carla, for he was afraid their time together was short.

The morning sky was clear, the water gentle, and the gondolier poled the boat smoothly to the landing a short walk away from San Zanipolo. He was the son of a gondolier who steered Carla for many years at the Courtesans' Boat Promenade and had brought her to and from assignations when her days and nights were full of lovers. His father, besotted with Carla's youthful beauty, always treated her with a respect beyond her rank. He sat her in the left seat of the felze, the seat of honor, no matter the status of her companion. He never cursed in her presence even when other gondoliers scraped or passed his boat too closely. He was true to the code of his calling: he kept secret where she went, who paid her a visit, or who shared her company in a curtained felze. The son, like any man with good eyes and a bit of imagination, saw why his father had been infatuated with Carla. Out of loyalty to his aged father he treated her with the courtesy owed a noblewoman. He grasped her arm gently and helped her out of the gondola. Rather than seek other passengers while they were in Zanipolo, he waited for them at the landing.

Bigio saw reflected in Carla's careful, painful steps his own frailty and mortality. A man didn't think of how much he had aged until he saw himself mirrored in the creased faces and stooped shoulders of his old friends. Carla paused inside the entrance of the church. "I've heard they are building cities in the New World where only bears and wild animals have lived. Stefano, is that true?"

He nodded his head yes.

"How sad to live in a place without the dead."

She was right. To live among strangers in a strange land where there was no shared past was a frightening thought. It would be like floating on the ocean and never being able to drop anchor.

"To live with the dead is to live with God," Carla said.

The tombs of the doges lined the walls of Zanipolo. Their bodies were brought here to be celebrated not mourned. The immense interior was bathed in a gentle pink light, the aisles were wide and tall, and the gleaming white marble columns swept away death's oppressive shadow. Carla sat on a marble bench jutting out from the wall to catch her breath and take in the quiet power of the place. She pointed across the church to the Valiero tomb.

Bigio decided to take a circular path past other tombs and monuments to postpone confronting the unpleasant presence of Silvestro and Elisabetta. Doge Loredan who with diplomatic skill overcame the betrayals of the Papacy, Marco Corner who helped suppress the attempted coup by the reviled Marino Faliero, Giovanni Dolfin who lost an eye in service to the Republic and despite his victory over the king of Hungary lay in a modest sarcophagus in a small chapel, and Michele Steno, victor against Padua, as modest in death as he was triumphant in life, rested as well in a simple tomb.

Others like the Mocenigo doges forever revered for their military victories were entombed with greater grandeur. Carlo over the Genoese and the Turks at Gallipoli, Giovanni at sea against Mehmed II and on land against the Duke of Ferrara, Alvise over the Ottomans at Lepanto, and Pietro victorious in Cyprus. Hercules slayed the Lernaean hydra and the Nemean Lion at the base of Pietro Mocenigo's monument, while he in military garment and pose stood atop a sarcophagus borne on the shoulders of three vanquished warriors. His victories over the Turks at Scutari and Famagusta were carved in relief on the sarcophagus, flanked on either side by another six defeated warriors. In the center of the sarcophagus was a carved inscription that Bigio read aloud to refresh his dusty Latin, *Ex hostium Manibus.* "From the hands of my enemies." Literally and figuratively, the tomb was built upon the backs of the Turks. The Mocenigos, political animals and patriots, wanted patrician and citizen to know that this magnificence in marble came not from the Republic's treasury but from the booty of the defeated.

For all its martial magnificence Pietro Mocenigo's tomb paled in comparison to the opulence and immensity of the Valiero tomb that took up an entire bay on the south side of the church, towering more than sixty feet from the floor to the vaulting. A third of the way up the tomb the three life-size Valieros stood like actors on a stage in front of an enormous yellow marble drape with a decorative floral pattern. Four putti strained to hold up the heavy drape crumpled like an unmade bed sheet. Doge Bertuccio Valiero, a smaller figure whose short reign was marked by his own ill health and the Republic's sickly state, stood between his son and daughter-in-law. Silvestro looked left toward his father and Elisabetta as if seeking their approval. He clutched in his right hand a pair of gloves. No sword, no instrument of power, no symbol of authority, just a pair of limp gloves.

Elisabetta, the marble equal of the two doges, grim faced, thick-necked, and wrinkled, glowered stiff backed on the right, covered from shoulders to feet with carved ruff, fur, lace, embroidery, and jewels. The sculptor threw up his hands, his artifice defeated by her vanity and ugliness. It was difficult to tell what was more creased and crinkled, her rumpled gown or her face and neck bound by a choker. Her hair in stiff ringlets jutted from her head like the serpents of Medusa. She had the double chin of someone who long pulled her head back to look down on the world and its lowly subjects. Beneath her, two putti held up a cloth of black marble with her epitaph chiseled in gold letters: *Elisabetta Querini. The wife of Silvestro, Distinguished by Roman virtue, By Venetian piety, And by the Ducal crown, Died 1708.* Were there no Venetian virtues? And what piety? Her life was marked by pride and the pursuit of worldly glory. No ash cloth and virtuous abnegation for her. She built this tomb for her husband and father-in-law, whose bones she moved from their initial resting place in the church. It was her life's last display of excess and pride. She was indeed distinguished by the ducal crown. That claim was true. It was a crown she bought and so flaunted that the Great Council made sure no dogaressa ever again would be allowed such pomp and power.

Elisabetta claimed in death the virtues she and Silvestro didn't embody in life. Between and below the two pairs of black marble columns that flanked the three Valieros were gathered all the stock characters of the funerary stage thrown together in a stew of false taste and self-adulation. Knowledge, Valor, Fortitude, Charity, and Meekness were among the Virtues dragooned to serve Elisabetta's vanity. Beneath Bertuccio, Virtue crowned Merit who, elderly, bearded, and beleaguered seemed on the edge of death. Anything heavier than the olive wreath Virtue placed on his head and he would have expired from the weight. Beneath this pitiful scene, another tableau celebrated the naval victory of Venice over the Turks at the Battle of the Dardanelles barely two weeks after Bertuccio's election, much too soon for him to claim the credit. Victory crowned the lion of the Republic as it leapt upon a vanquished dragon. With furrowed brow and raised forepaws, the sad-eyed lion looked like a dog begging for a bone. It seemed to Bigio that the sculptor, who didn't lack skill, couldn't bring himself to embrace Elisabetta's false claim of martial prowess for her father-in-law.

Sunlight raked through stained glass and illuminated the church in soft light, but the prideful extravagance and self-congratulation of the Valieros darkened Bigio's mood. Venice was dying, and this hulking cliff of marble tastelessness was a symptom of its terminal condition. The glory of the Republic lay buried with these hollow bones. It was a dissolute age. Wealth had deposed character. Display had dethroned dignity. He stepped back from this unintended monument to the Republic's decline to get one last view. An old woman in widow's black shuffled past to light a candle in the front of the carved relief of Charity. Her shoes were cracked and split. Bigio saw her calloused heels where the threaded seam had come loose. A wisp of smoke spiraled upward past the child slumbering at Charity's feet to the infant suckling at her marble breast. Bigio looked again at the tomb towering in front of him. This must have cost a king's ransom he said out loud to himself, and in the saying he knew.

Behind the golden drapery lay the Querini's dirty secret and Zampelli's sin. *Ex hostium Manibus.* There were no defeated enemies, no plunder from the vanquished. *Ex sacerdos Manibus.* From the hands of the priest, from the pockets of the parishioners. This tomb with all its marble drapery, statues, and sculpted reliefs was built on the backs of innocent parishioners who thought they were sacrificing for the glory of Saint Pantalon. The money Zampelli paid for the care of his son was a pittance compared to what he and other priests embezzled to build this tainted monument to Elisabetta's vanity and pride. Bigio turned around and walked across the vast nave toward Carla. She looked at him and nodded her head slowly up and down. He was certain she knew. He needed some fresh air. He felt unclean. He needed a basin of cool water and a damp cloth to wash away the stench.

44

Bigio heard a faint tapping at the shuttered window. He opened the shutter slowly. On the window ledge sat St. Jude, or at least it looked like his old, sad companion. What other bird would want to live in such drab surroundings and suffer such meager fare? The forlorn bird looked at Bigio as if to beg his permission to return. Bigio motioned toward the empty cage, its sliding panel left open. The sparrow flew across the room into its old home. Bigio wanted to believe he came back for the company, though likely he gave up fighting for bits of bread and scraps of garbage with the pigeons that ruled the cobblestones and roofs of the Republic. Better a few crumbs of stale bread than starvation.

"Welcome back my friend. You were missed. You must excuse me. I have important business to attend to. If all goes well, soon you will feast on more than water bugs and cockroaches." Bigio looked at his feathered companion. "You're right, friends come first." Bigio swept some breadcrumbs from the table and scattered them at the bottom of Jude's cage.

"Preparation and strategy, St. Jude."

Bigio sat at the table, the gray light of dusk seeping through the shutters. He rehearsed what he would say to Zampelli in the morning, sometimes talking out loud, sometimes tapping a spoon on the table to emphasize the point he was making silently to himself. "What Jude? A firmer voice? I will try again." Bigio was used to the evasions of politeness but not to lying. He didn't want a hesitant word, an awkward pause, or an obvious inconsistency to betray him. Bigio still remembered the sting of his father's belt and the shame he felt those many years ago. He asked his father for forgiveness this one time. He wanted the money.

"After tomorrow, my friend, we will both eat better."

45

Bigio waited at a table outside a café in Campo Santa Margherita. For a brief moment he thought of having Zampelli come to his room after early morning mass to confront him with the straitened condition of his life. That would have been demeaning, no better than shaking a beggar's bowl in his face. He didn't want to meet in the sacristy, Zampelli's own terrain, where he would feel comfortable, better able to lie again. Instead Bigio sat with his back to the market so the priest would be forced to take the chair facing Pietro's stand where his pregnant widow and young daughter were working. Zampelli waddled to the table and glanced at Pietro's widow as he sat down.

"She hopes it will be a son," Bigio said. "She will call him Pietro."

The priest didn't say anything. He looked pained, as Bigio hoped he would be. A boy brought coffee, while the priest talked awkwardly about the uncommonly good weather. Bigio sipped his coffee and nodded, stretching out the uncomfortable silence that hovered between them.

"You'll not like what I have to say, but God likes the truth. You know I am a bit of a Philistine when it comes to painting. I went through Fumiani's drawings quickly. Angels and saints, a hand here or there, a muscled back, even a horse's flank. They were just the idle scribbles of an old man. When I was ill after Pietro's death and too weak to even read a bit of Dante, as I sometimes like to do, I decided to look again at the journals. Folded among the pages were some loose sheets of writing that I had overlooked, written with what appeared to be a quick, urgent hand." Bigio paused, his right hand twisting the fingers of his left hand under the table until the fingertips turned red. "Lucio da Nove was murdered. Fumiani saw it with his own eyes. It wasn't an accident."

Zampelli shook his head. "I can't believe it," he mumbled.

"Fumiani was haunted by da Nove's death and blamed himself," Bigio continued calmly, weaving what he hoped was a convincing skein of lies. "He thought that there wasn't enough contrast in the beheading scene, the executioner's sword lost among the background browns and greens. The sword needed to glint in the light. Da Nove said it looked good to him, but if Fumiani insisted, he would go back up after the parishioners lit their last candles and said their last prayers of the day. Fumiani had bought some flowers for Laura but left them at the church. Halfway home he returned to retrieve them from a small room off the sacristy. He entered quietly, unnoticed in the dim light. Da Nove had borrowed Fumiani's smock. He stood on the small scaffold on the right side of the working ceiling built over the nave. His back was to the church entrance. He was singing to himself as he worked, something he often did. He didn't hear the two men, their faces covered with masks, climbing the scaffold. Before he could turn around and disclose his true identity, they grabbed him and hurled him off the scaffold. Fumiani wasn't sure they even knew they killed the wrong man. Fumiani fled in fear, ashamed at his cowardice for not coming to the aid of a good man, guilty for asking him to do what he should have done himself and what in his quest for perfection need not have been done at all."

Zampelli's face collapsed like a Carnival puppet whose strings have been cut. "Why would anyone want to kill Fumiani?"

Bigio looked directly at Zampelli, knowing now more than ever he had to maintain a grim demeanor and convincing tone. "He knew about you."

"I didn't have anything to do with da Nove's death. You know I would never do anything to harm Fumiani."

"He knew. Cassana told him."

"Cassana? The painter? Told him what? I don't understand. Everyone knows that man has a wicked tongue."

Cassana was in England out of revenge's way. Bigio wove him into the tale. Even if he were still in Venice, no one would dare antagonize the Medicis and their allies. "One night, Cassana came to Fumiani's studio to negotiate a commission for the Grand Prince. He had drunk one or two glasses of wine too many. His tongue was looser and more poisonous than usual. Fumiani was preparing a large canvas with white gesso. Better you paint it first and whiten it afterwards, Cassana said with a vicious laugh. Cassana knew Fumiani needed the money, and he drove a hard bargain. When Fumiani complained, he told him he should take what the Prince was so generously offering. Haven't you ever wondered why it is taking so long for Pantalon to be rebuilt he asked in a taunting tone. Are you the last one in the city to know that Elisabetta Querini has been squeezing money from the priest at Pantalon for years to make sure her husband was elected doge and, now that he's dead, to build a tomb grander than any other in Zanipolo?"

"Fumiani never said a word to me. He knew it was a lie."

"He didn't have time," Bigio said. "Or maybe he didn't believe it or want to believe it. You gave him the opportunity to paint his masterpiece. What a troubled soul he must have been thinking if he confronted you, he might lose his chance to stand shoulder to shoulder with the giants of the past?" Bigio held up his hand up to stop Zampelli from lying again. "It really doesn't matter if Fumiani spoke to you or not. Someone thought he would. Someone thought he knew too much. Maybe another night after Cassana had too much to drink, his loose tongue let slip what he told Fumiani. This is a Republic of spies. Someone friendly to the Querinis heard his boast. Someone thought it was time the painting was finished."

Zampelli's hands were shaking. "I had nothing to do with the murder. Nothing, you must believe me."

"I want to believe you're not that base a man. But you stole from the church, and your embezzling was the cause of an innocent man's death." Bigio turned and looked toward Pietro's stall. "Two men's death."

"I wasn't the only one."

"You're the only one that matters to me."

"Stefano, they were loans."

"Did she pay them back?'

"No, she didn't have time."

A person believed what he had to believe to be the person he thought he was. Zampelli believed it was a loan, even if all reason argued against it. Otherwise he was damned even in his own eyes. "Well now it's time. It's time for the Querinis to pay what they owe."

"I will send money to da Nove's wife and make sure Pietro's wife and child are taken care of. I promise."

"Father, I will take care of them." Bigio told Zampelli how much he wanted.

Zampelli's hands trembled. "My god, Stefano. That is more than enough. They aren't the widows of patricians."

Bigio repeated the amount.

"Where I am going to get that kind of money?"

"That's your problem. I won't ask questions and don't care as long as it comes from those who can afford to pay. Not from the pockets of the parish."

It was an amount large enough to pay those who needed to be paid but not so large that the Querinis couldn't gather it up in a week's time. "Please tell those with blood on their hands that I've put down in writing everything I've told you and given it and Fumiani's papers to a man of great reputation. If I die a suspicious death, he has instructions to give everything to the Council of Ten."

Zampelli crossed his arms atop the table and lowered his head.

He couldn't look Bigio in the eyes. "Don't you want to know why I did it?"

"I'm not here to take your confession."

"I didn't do it for myself. I did it for the church, for the parish. She promised they would help pay for the marble façade. I couldn't raise that much money. Comino's plans are glorious but beyond the means of the parish. They would pay back what they borrowed and more. I helped her to help the church." His eyes began to tear. He sniffled and ran his hand across his nose. "I'll die before the church is finished. I will never see the new façade."

Bigio got no pleasure from seeing Zampelli suffer but said nothing to ease his pain. Zampelli had to pay. He betrayed the poor of the parish. He betrayed Fumiani. Pietro died because of a weak man and a vain woman. Elisabetta's grandiose designs were well beyond the money Silvestro left in his will for his tomb. Pietro died because a priest was more in love with glorifying God for his own vanity than for God himself and Pantalon, his holy martyr. A priest deceived by appearances, by a façade of marble, let a woman in Nove live four years in darkness hobbled by hope. All for a self-important woman's sad, grubby obsession with power and her overweening pride. Power sought for no grand purpose, no worthy motives that Bigio could see, just personal pleasure and the pomp of the office. Power for its own sake, like a gambler at the Ridotto addicted to the dice, not for the money but for the thrill of the action. Bribery, electoral corruption, and the free flow of money and favors didn't shock Bigio. After all, this was Venice. Beneath the city's marble magnificence the salt water rotted the pilings. Bigio was too old for illusions. More people suffered and died in this world from the petty passions of the powerful than in service to a great cause. Now all that mattered was the money.

47

Carla untied the leather packet. "What is all of this?"

"My promise."

Her hand trembled as she leafed through the bank documents in her name. "Stefano, have you become a thief in your old age? Where did this all money come from?"

"It is a gift. A gift from the grave." He smiled, "You were right, Elisabetta was a very generous woman."

"I will have to live to be a hundred to spend all this money."

He pointed a finger toward the ceiling, "I will be watching."

"Quiet, don't speak like that."

"Well, if you would like, you can always treat me to a good cup of coffee once in a while."

At her asking, Bigio told her about Zampelli's embezzlement for Elisabetta and the money he gave to Lucio da Nove and Pietro's widows.

"Dear Stefano, I am proud of you."

"I had no choice, the dead demanded it. Debts have to be paid."

"Poor Pietro. His death was so unnecessary. His wife and child..."

"Elisabetta, contemned in life, was dead and forgotten. It was a stupid mistake by hotheaded Flavio Querini who didn't understand the way the world worked. You know, Carla, Fumiani has taught me a lot about the power of illusion. We look up at his painting, and we think we are in heaven, but we are still in the fallen world below. Young, dimwitted Flavio was lost in illusion. He wanted to preserve the reputation of a family whose name was already stained beyond redemption."

"Stefano, I know all about illusion. This is a city of secrets and illusions. I'm an angel of illusion."

"But you are a beautiful illusion. The Republic is a decaying corpse whose citizens think it's healthy and vigorous. Oh, maybe a scratch or cut here and there, but it's a hearty and vital body with a virtuous soul. They are living in a nightmare of corruption but will themselves not to see it. They close their eyes and believe they are living in a heavenly dream."

"You haven't told tell the Council, have you?"

"I suspect the Council knew of the embezzlement behind Silvestro's election and his tomb and had buried the truth with the doge and his disgraced wife. If they didn't, you and I know there's a limit to what a poor patrician can do in Venice. The embezzlement was in the past, of no consequence now to the Council or anyone. No use denouncing the dead. Even Hercules couldn't clean out the muck and corruption of these stables. The machinations of the Broglio are constant as the tides, the stench of power as fetid as the canals' stink in summer. I don't want to be a hero. All I want is a good night's sleep and not to lay awake thinking I'm part of the corruption."

"What about denouncing the living?"

He nodded yes. "I've denounced Flavio Querini for ordering Pietro's murder. The Admiral and Sagredo signed the denunciation as witnesses."

"I see why the Admiral would do it, but why Sagredo, a man you've only met once?"

"He says I'm a changed man. That I've learned to look up."

The Querinis would sacrifice Flavio. Even before Pietro's murder, he was a hot-tempered embarrassment to the family. He didn't have a future worth defending. They would say he drank too much, had a grudge – bought a rotten peach or some other lie – but no word of the embezzlement. What the Council would do,

Bigio didn't know, exile most likely. For a man like Flavio, whose only power lay in his name, exile to some small Dalmatian island where he would be a nobody would be for him a punishment worse than death.

Carla still didn't understand what happened that fatal day in the church. "I almost believed the web of lies I wove to catch Zampelli," Bigio said. "Maybe it was just a slip of the foot, a loose plank, a sudden dizzy spell by a tired man. Remember Carla, it was you who chided me for trying to explain everything."

"An accident for da Nove but what of Fumiani? Why did he run away? Now that I am a rich woman, a *denari* for your thoughts. Tell me what you think happened, Stefano."

Bigio wove another tale with the drama that he knew Carla wanted. A well-told tale not to deceive but to explain to her and to himself what may have happened. "May have," he cautioned. The Electress went home to Bavaria, her praise echoed by everyone who came to San Pantalon that day. But Fumiani wasn't satisfied. He knew the ceiling could be better. Fumiani walked back and forth on the floor below: he wanted to amaze and overwhelm the faithful with heavenly illusion from any place they stood. The planking, removed so the Electress could view the ceiling, was put back. It supported a smaller, mobile scaffold that Fumiani moved from figure to figure in the spandrels between the windows. Every day he climbed up and down the scaffolding to make sure that the brushwork that appeared rough and coarse up close looked harmonious and pleasing from below. He wanted all the figures that floated in heaven and extended out from the walls to look alive and in motion, not flat like cheap opera scenery. Fumiani ordered da Nove back up the scaffolding another "one last time." Da Nove, who soon would return to his wife and child, had worked all day after a night of little sleep and too much wine celebrating his time in Venice coming to an end. He hurriedly grabbed Fumiani's paint-splattered smock, climbed up the ladders to the platform, and moved the scaffold to where Fumiani wanted it. "Just a bit more," Fumiani yelled up to him. The planks had been moved back and forth for the Electress. A plank shifted under the weight of the scaffold. The small, unstable scaffold tottered, and da Nove tumbled headfirst to the floor. Fumiani ran quickly to the body and knew without turning him over that that he was dead.

"Here, I jump into deepest part of the ocean where the bottom lies miles below in darkness. Fumiani looked down as his crimson smock and da Nove's head pooled in blood, a martyr to his own obsession with perfection. He shouldn't have sent him up again. He should have taken more care with the scaffolding. Fumiani didn't run out into the campo for help or back into the sacristy to find Zampelli. He walked stiffly like a sleepwalker up and down the nave in the fading light and stared at the ceiling, arching his neck, looking up at the trials of Saint Pantalon and the soles of angels. Emperor Maximian's unfeeling gaze mocked him. The ceiling blurred into a swirling mass of brown and yellows. Heaven's glow seemed more distant than ever. All the years had come to nothing. There were no miracles in San Pantalon. He turned and walked from the church, leaving da Nove's body and his own life behind."

"Oh Stefano, what a sad man. Is it true?"

"I don't know. The pieces fit, but we will never know unless God turns ashes back to ink and paper."

"It's a glorious painting," Carla said.

"Not to him. It wasn't what he hoped it would be. It was done, but he hadn't reached where he wanted to go. No more illusion. There was no one to blame. Not Laura and her shallow dreams, not Zampelli and his delays. He saw the Promised Land, but he knew his brush would never bring him there. He would die in the land of Moab and that ate at his soul."

"But he was a good painter," Carla's voice quivered with sorrow. "Couldn't he see that?"

"He was a good painter not a great one. For someone with his ambition, falling short of greatness by an inch was like standing at the far edge of a wide chasm. He reached for God's hand and touched only air."

Carla sat silently, staring at her gloved hands trembling lightly in her lap. "Poor Fumiani. His art didn't save him like Fra Lippi, did it?"

"No, it didn't. He looked up one last time at the angels in heaven. He knew in his despair something was missing. He had an artist's eye, an artist's hand but a craftsman's soul. He saw the game was up, threw his cards down, and left the table."

"And left his wife?"

"They had left each other long before. He was tired of being Fumiani."

"Stefano, he could never escape himself. None of us can." Carla patted the space on the settee next to her. "Enough of Fumiani for tonight. Come sit next to me. Let me read from dear Petrarch."

The words always mattered less to Bigio than the intimacy of Carla's voice. She read with a sensuous hush that enveloped him like soft wool. He always found the poet's obsession with a woman he had barely spoken to, if at all, a bit unmanly. She was an idealized woman made more beautiful and alluring by the distance between them. He seduced himself by the power of his own words. He was tired of men besotted with illusion. Fumiani once looked at the face of his Laura and thought her an angel fallen to earth into his arms. In the end he realized she was an illusion, that her beauty had deceived him. Fumiani once thought himself a master of illusion, now he knew illusion was his master.

"Not today. No words. Your company is comfort enough."

48

Lucio da Nove, an itinerant workman at San Pantalon, told Giovanni Fumiani that he would be leaving for home in a few days now that the painting was finished. He was ready to return to his wife and son. He had been away too long. He would find work in Nove and in the villages nearby. There was always need for a man good with his hands. There was always a nearby village church that needed repair.

Da Nove handed Fumiani a small drawing to thank him for the work. Fumiani held the sheet in his hands without saying a word. The silence embarrassed da Nove. It was nothing, he said, just something to pass the time. An old woman he saw one day in the Chapel of Saint Ann. How did he do it? Fumiani asked. Da Nove shook his head. He didn't know. He just picked up a piece of chalk and out came the head, the mouth, the eyes. A simple mechanical, he never studied with any master and hadn't a scrap of formal training about the laws and rules of perspective. What he knew he couldn't put into words. But the arm, Fumiani said, it didn't look right. It was out of proportion to the rest of the old woman's body. The workman looked down, not sure what to say, afraid he might offend the master painter. Yes, he said, but it felt right. Fumiani looked more closely at the old woman's arm as she lit the candle. It worked. Da Nove had wandered into the Promised Land without even wanting to.

Fumiani said the ceiling wasn't finished. He wanted da Nove to stay a little bit longer. Fumiani wasn't satisfied with the scourging of San Pantalon. The scene needed to come alive. The color needed to be more vibrant. The flesh was too much like polished marble. Fumiani wanted the faithful to cringe in anticipation of the blow. He wanted the faithful to hear the serpent's tongue of the hooded priest hunched over Pantalon's shoulder trying to seduce him into renouncing his faith. Stay for a few more weeks, Lucio. Just a few more weeks, Fumiani said, and it would be perfect.

49

The white marble of Redentore glowed against a blue, cloudless Venetian sky. Bigio looked across the Giudecca Canal at the city etched against the blue and could almost believe in the goodness of his fellow man. Almost. This city across the canal with all its glories was a vast *memento mori*. The lapping water ate away the pilings of the fondamenta. His nieces lost the Bigio name in marriage. When he died, the name would become a fading memory and disappear. Bigio would leave no mark. He would die only once. Fumiani died twice and would die once more, and the poor haunted man knew it. Artists honored a century ago were names now rarely spoken and little remembered. It was as if they never had lifted a brush, as if they had never lived. Dante was right: "Your renown is but the hue of grass, which comes and goes, and the same sun that makes it spring green from the ground will wither it." A few, a very few, were venerated by every age. Most were forgotten in a generation. Fumiani lay on his narrow bed at the other end of the Giudecca wondering if any future chronicler of the city would mention San Pantalon. If he did, would his readers purse their lips and shake their heads trying to loosen from their cobwebbed brains the name of the artist who toiled for almost twenty years on a painting they saw once as a child and had forgotten. Old women would shuffle into San Pantalon their eyes tracing steps across the marble floor. Voluptuaries stalked by guilt and images of the inferno would come to confess their sins and ask for absolution so they could sin again in flesh and folly. Few would bend their necks back and look up at the ceiling darkened with smoke and inattention. Some future Vasari with his book of third-hand tales might not even mention his name when writing of the city's treasures. Or worse, he would drop his name in passing on his journey to a more acclaimed artist, Fumiani's work a deserted village off the main road to the capital.

Bigio walked slowly up the stairs of Redentore. He was alone in the church, only he and God. His cane echoed against the clean coolness of unpainted walls and ceiling. There were no tombs here. The Capuchin friars who gave up the site for the church refused to allow any extravagant displays of vanity and self-adulation as there were in Zanipolo. Just white walls and sunlight. Here Bigio felt at peace, almost healed, as if he could stand up and walk straight without halt or limp.

Bigio stood where Fumiani could well have stood. The human soul with all its hidden crevices and chambers could never be known, except by God. No man could fully decipher the mystery of another man's life. Yet Bigio now knew why Fumiani walked along the canal all the way to Redentore. Not for the view, not out of nostalgia for his old life across the canal. He came for the possibilities. He came for the white walls and unpainted ceiling and another chance at salvation.

Bigio limped down the stairs into a cloudless day more beautiful than the fine gloss of memory could ever fashion. So beautiful that he almost believed there could be white walls and clean slates. It was good to think there could be, even if only for a moment.

He walked down the fondamenta toward the landing. A gondola was approaching. It was Thursday. Carla was waiting.

III

The Third Death of Giovanni Fumiani

"It is notable that little of what was produced in Venice in the seventeenth century is actually looked at today, even by an informed visitor."
John Steer, *Venetian Painting: A Concise History* (1970)

Acknowledgements

First and foremost, to Martha Hoffman for her faith in the novel and for her thoughtful editing that has made it a much better work. To Maya Slouka whose insightful review of an early draft identified issues to address. To my late friend Robert Bledsoe for his recommendation that I read Robert Browning's poem "Andrea del Sarto" and the thematic inspiration it provided. And as always to my wife Mee-Seen Loong for her patience and support.

CPSIA information can be obtained
at www.ICGtesting.com
Printed in the USA
JSHW012130190123
36538JS00002B/95